Growing up near the beach, **Annie West** spent lots of time observing tall, burnished lifeguards—early research! Now she spends her days fantasising about gorgeous men and their love-lives. Annie has been a reader all her life. She also loves travel, long walks, good company and great food. You can contact her at annie@annie-west.com or via PO Box 1041, Warners Bay, NSW 2282, Australia.

Also by Annie West

Contracted for the Petrakis Heir
Inherited for the Royal Bed
Her Forgotten Lover's Heir
The Greek's Forbidden Innocent
Revelations of a Secret Princess

Passion in Paradise collection

Wedding Night Reunion in Greece

Royal Brides for Desert Brothers miniseries

Sheikh's Royal Baby Revelation
Demanding His Desert Queen

Discover more at millsandboon.co.uk.

CONTRACTED TO HER GREEK ENEMY

ANNIE WEST

MILLS & BOON

First Published in Great Britain 2020
by Mills & Boon, an imprint of HarperCollins*Publishers*
1 London Bridge Street, London, SE1 9GF

© 2020 Annie West

ISBN: 978-0-263-08846-5

MIX
Paper from
responsible sources
FSC® C007454

This book is produced from independently certified FSC™ paper
to ensure responsible forest management.
For more information visit www.harpercollins.co.uk/green.

Printed and bound in Great Britain
by CPI Group (UK) Ltd, Croydon, CR0 4YY

This is my 40th book for Harlequin Mills and Boon!

Celebrations are in order, and thanks:

To the readers who enjoy my stories. You've made my dream of writing romance come true.

To my terrific editor Carly Byrne.

To my writer friends, especially Anna Campbell, Abby Green, Michelle Douglas and Cathryn Hein.

To Efthalia Pegios for advice on Greek.

To my wonderful family.

This book is dedicated to my mum.

CHAPTER ONE

'I'VE HAD ENOUGH, DAMEN. I can't stand it any more. I feel like running away.'

Damen's eyebrows rose. Clio wasn't the sort to run from trouble. 'It can't be that bad.'

Wrong response, Nicolaides!

Even before she flashed him an outraged glare, Damen realised his mistake. With a mother and two younger sisters, he had a healthy respect for feminine temper. Clearly this was serious.

'Oh, can't it?' She shook her head and her diamond drop earrings swung. 'He's not just badgering me, but Mama too. It's his only topic of conversation. I don't dare show my face or call Mama because it sets him off again.'

She hefted a shuddery breath and Damen was horrified as he watched tears well. He'd never seen his cousin Clio cry. And though they were only second cousins, they were as close as siblings.

Clio's chin wobbled. 'It's Cassie's wedding soon but I'm not sure I can face going to it. My own little sister's wedding!'

Damen's gut churned. Clio was hurting and *he* was responsible. He should have realised—

'All my father does is rave about how *I* as the eldest should be marrying first. How you and I are a perfect match and how selfish I am not settling down with the man who's decent, honourable and suitable in every way.' She bit her lip and slanted him a glance. 'Of course, he never mentions how suitable your fortune is.'

That flash of humour didn't ease the dark cloud settling over Damen's conscience.

This was no joke. Manos was a difficult man at the best

of times and he could make life hell for Clio and her whole family.

Damen grabbed her hand, felt it tremble and cursed himself for putting her in this situation. Once Manos got an idea it was almost impossible to shift it.

'I'm sorry, Clio. This is all down to me. I should never—'

'*Don't* go all macho and say it's your fault, Damen Nicolaides! I know you're used to shouldering responsibility for everyone, but you're not solely to blame.' She sighed. 'We both are. You think I haven't enjoyed going to all those A-list parties with you? You think I haven't been networking like mad, building up a list of potential clients for my business?'

'It was my idea.' Because he'd tired of fending off women who wanted more from him than a mutually satisfying fling. No matter how often he said he wasn't in the market for the long term, they thought they could change his mind.

With Clio as his semi-regular date things had been much easier. His occasional lovers were more accepting of the fact he wasn't shopping for a wife.

A cold shiver started at his nape and crawled down his spine at the word, chilling each vertebra as it went.

Gentle fingers squeezed his hand. 'You did nothing wrong, Damen.'

He focused on Clio's earnest face and wondered if she was talking about this issue with her father or the past, when clearly Damen *had* been to blame. Typical of Clio to try to absolve him.

She'd stood by him when he'd really needed it. She deserved better than this mess.

'Okay, let's agree neither of us were at fault.' They were adults, entitled to socialise together, even if they weren't and never would be lovers. 'That still leaves the problem of your father. We have to find a way to disabuse him of his expectations without him blaming you.'

Clio pulled her hand away, smoothing it down the silk dress she wore for today's celebration.

'I tell you, I'm running away. To Tierra del Fuego.'

Damen heard despair beneath that light-hearted tone.

'Do you even know where that is?'

'Okay, then, the Arctic Circle. I'll branch into interior design for igloos.'

Despite himself, Damen laughed. His cousin could do it too. She was a talented designer, up for any challenge.

Except getting herself out of this mess. It would take more than Clio's word to convince Manos she and Damen weren't an item. Especially with the prize of Damen's vast fortune in the equation. Which it always was.

That was one of the prime reasons he'd resorted to 'dates' with his cousin, to stave off the women angling to snare a rich husband. A Greek billionaire with no wife and a healthy cash flow despite the recent economic troubles was a catch. One in his early thirties with a full head of hair and all his own teeth was a rarity.

'Forget the igloos and leave this to me.'

'You have an idea?' No mistaking the hope in her tone.

Damen nodded. 'The beginnings of one. But give me time to sort out the details. Trust me, I'll sort Manos.'

Relief eased her tight expression. 'Thanks, Damen. I should have realised I could count on you.'

Twenty minutes later, Damen stood beside his best friend, Christo, who was to marry today. Christo was checking his phone, leaving Damen free to admire the panoramic view of the sea off Corfu. But Damen ignored the vista, instead surveying the guests gathered in the villa's garden.

What he needed was a woman. And quickly.

A woman to play the part of his lover long enough to persuade Manos that Damen and Clio had no future together.

If he attended the upcoming wedding of Clio's sister, Cassie, with a striking new girlfriend in tow, that would dent Manos's hopes. If Damen kept that new girlfriend with him for a couple of months, his very public companion...

But which woman?

Someone single. And attractive, for Manos was no fool. There had to be a sizzle of desire between Damen and his new companion.

But Damen needed someone who wouldn't see this as an opportunity to angle for a real relationship. A woman who wouldn't try to win his affections and carve out a place for herself in his life.

'Relax.' Christo's voice interrupted his thoughts. 'I'm the one getting married, not you.'

Damen flashed his old friend a smile. 'And marrying the same woman twice. That's some sort of record.'

Christo shrugged and spread his hands. 'The first time I had no idea how much she meant to me. This time everything is perfect between us. I just hope you find a woman like Emma one day. A woman who's the centre of your world, the love of your life.'

Damen's smile solidified. As if he believed in that any more! For others, if they were extraordinarily lucky, but not himself. He'd lost his naivety a decade ago.

Ruthlessly he yanked his thoughts from the events that had changed him, and his family, for ever. Today was a joyous day, not one for dwelling on mistakes and tragedy.

Damen retrieved two glasses of champagne from a passing waiter and passed one to his best friend. 'Here's to you and your lovely Emma. And,' he added when they'd both sipped their wine, 'here's to me finding my own perfect woman.'

One who was attractive, intelligent, amenable and, above all, expendable.

'You look stunning, Emma.' Steph finished pinning the antique lace veil in place and stepped back. She'd never seen her best friend so happy. She positively glowed.

Emma grinned. 'You've seen the outfit before.'

It was the one she'd worn the first time she married

Christo, before she deserted him on learning he didn't love her. So much had happened since, but miraculously, in that time Emma and her Greek billionaire husband had sorted out their differences. They were so much in love it almost hurt to look at such joy.

'Hey, Steph, what is it? Are you sure you're okay?'

Instantly guilt crowded in. Emma was too sharp. She'd taken one look at Steph when she stepped off the plane at Corfu Airport and asked what was wrong. Persuading Emma that she was fine, just tired after the trip from Melbourne, had taken all Steph's skill.

Steph refused to mar Emma's big day with her woes. She'd find a solution to the fix she was in, though every avenue she'd pursued so far had proved a dead end. She'd just have to try harder.

Because this trouble didn't affect her alone. She suppressed a shiver.

'Of course I'm okay! Can't I just be a little emotional, seeing you so radiant? You look like a fairy princess.'

For a second she read doubt in Emma's expression before it was ousted by another smile. 'I *feel* like one! Pinch me so I know this is real.'

Steph didn't pinch her, but she did hug her, hard. 'I'm so happy for you, Em. You deserve this after all you've been through.'

'If it's a matter of deserving...' Emma stepped back, shaking her head and clearly intending to say more, but Steph stopped her.

'Come on, Em, it's time to get this show on the road.'

Emma gasped when she saw the time and turned to the door in a flurry of long skirts. Steph twitched the veil into place and followed her out into the warm Greek sunshine.

It was a glorious day in a perfect setting. The garden of the gracious old villa made a wonderful wedding venue, with the stunning blue-green sea as a backdrop. But what made the event so special was the sight of her dear friend committing herself to the man she loved.

Yet now, as Steph mingled with the well-wishers after the ceremony, she couldn't concentrate fully on this wonderful occasion. Not because of her own worries. They'd still be there later, crowding close again soon enough.

No, the buzz of discomfort came from *him*. The man who, every time she turned, was watching her. Even as he chatted with, it seemed, every female under forty at the reception.

Steph could trace his progress through the crowd, since he left behind a trail of starry-eyed women.

But not her.

Because the dark-haired man standing head and superb shoulders above the throng was Damen Nicolaides.

Snake.

Lowlife.

The man who'd conned her into making a fool of herself.

She felt sick when she thought of it.

She couldn't believe how simple it had been for him. Steph might be impulsive but when it came to men she'd learned almost from the cradle not to trust easily.

So why had she forgotten her hard-won lessons the moment Damen Nicolaides crooked his finger? She who'd never allowed herself to be swayed before by masculine charm and a sexy body.

Because she'd made the mistake of believing Damen was different. That he was loyal and caring. Which it appeared he was, for those he genuinely valued. Anyone outside that charmed circle had to be wary. For he was also devious, calculating and utterly ruthless.

The memory of that evening in Melbourne still haunted her when she let her defences down or when she was tired. Which was often, these days, as worry kept her awake most nights.

And why, oh, why had she allowed herself to be wrong-

footed by yet another plausible, smooth-talking male, even after her experience with demon Damen?

In her weaker moments Steph toyed with the idea that in succumbing to Damen's charm she'd somehow destroyed her defences and her judgement. Obviously it was now fatally flawed when it came to the opposite sex.

From now on she'd have nothing to do with them. It was safer that way.

At least with Damen it was only her feminine pride that had been bruised. Which led inevitably to thoughts of the catastrophe facing her back in Australia.

Anguish churned her insides. Suddenly she wasn't in the mood for celebrating.

Steph spied a path leading away from the villa. Picking up her long skirts, she followed it, only stopping when the sounds of celebration grew muted. She was at the top of a low cliff looking over a horseshoe beach of perfect white sand. The breeze brought the mingled scent of cypresses and the sea, and Steph drew a steadying breath.

She'd head back soon. Just take a few moments to recharge her batteries and overcome her maudlin thoughts. This was Emma's special day and Steph intended to be there for her.

'You're not enjoying the party?'

The voice slid through her like melted chocolate, smooth, rich and compelling. To her horror Steph felt something deep inside ease and loosen.

As if she'd been waiting for this.

She'd avoided speaking to Damen Nicolaides. Yet she'd know his voice anywhere. Not merely because she'd earlier heard the deep tone of his murmured conversation with Christo, but because she still heard him in her dreams.

Steph clenched her jaw and stood straighter. So he had a great voice, deep and luscious. She knew better than to be taken in by that.

'I wanted a breather. Some time alone.'

If she stared at the picture-postcard view long enough surely he'd get the message and leave.

Instead she heard the crunch of measured footsteps on gravel.

'Direct as ever, Stephanie.'

Steph bit her lip, hating the way that softening sensation spread, as if the man only had to speak and her female hormones got all fluttery and eager.

Just because no one else called her by her full name. Or made it sound like an invitation to sin.

Heat flared in her veins and shot to her cheeks.

'Then perhaps you'll take the hint and go back to the party.'

His only answer was a huff of amusement that rippled across her tight shoulders and nape. Instead of retreating, he stopped behind and to the side of her. She couldn't see him in her peripheral vision but sensed him. It was an awareness she couldn't explain and didn't want to.

'Here, I brought you a peace offering.'

A hand appeared before her, broad, olive-skinned, perfectly manicured. It held champagne in a crystal glass.

Steph was about to refuse when he continued. 'I thought we could toast the happy couple.'

It was the one thing that could persuade her to accept the drink. Did he know that?

Of course he did. He was smart, this man. Cunning. Steph recalled how easily he'd made her dance to his tune.

And you're only giving him more power now by letting him see that still bothers you.

Steph reached for the glass, careful not to touch those long fingers. She drew a deep breath, reluctantly inhaling that faint scent she remembered from before, a woodsy, warm, appealing aroma. Recognition skittered through her, a spurious sense of rightness. She ignored it and turned.

'To the bride and groom.' She lifted her glass and swallowed. Then took another long sip to ease the sudden dryness in her throat.

Up close he didn't look like a snake. He looked as handsome as ever. Honed cheekbones and a squared jaw that gave him an aura of determination. Long, straight nose, a sensual mouth and eyes of forest green that seemed to glint in the afternoon light. Dark hair that she knew to be soft to the touch.

Her fingers twitched and the glass jerked in her hold. Quickly she dipped her head and took another tiny sip.

'To Emma and Christo,' he murmured. 'May they be happy together for the rest of their lives.'

He drank and Steph found herself watching his throat work. As if there was something innately fascinating about the movement. When she lifted her gaze it meshed with his and awareness jolted through her.

No, no, no. Not awareness. This wasn't like last time. Dislike. Scorn. Disdain. Any of those would do.

'Thank you for the drink,' she said politely, as if to a complete stranger. There, that was better. Treat him like a stranger. 'Now, I'd better head back. Emma—'

'Is surrounded by excited friends and family. She can do without you a little longer.'

Steph's eyebrows rose. 'Nevertheless, it's time I returned.'

'I'd hoped we could talk.'

'Talk?' What could they possibly have to discuss? 'We have nothing to talk about.'

Was it her imagination or did that strong jaw clench? The gleam in those remarkable eyes dimmed and Steph had the impression, suddenly, that something serious lurked behind his air of assurance.

'About Melbourne—'

'There's nothing to discuss. It's in the past.'

'It doesn't feel like it. You look at me with hostility, Stephanie.'

Her fingers curled around the stem of the champagne glass as she fought the impulse to throw the rest of her drink over his too-handsome face.

Except she wouldn't make a scene at Emma's wedding.

Her eyes rounded in disbelief. 'You're surprised by that?'

'I apologised.'

'Oh, and that makes it all right, does it?' Steph waved her hand and vintage champagne arced through the air, splashing onto the ground.

'I did what was necessary to help my friend.'

'You *kidnapped* me!' Steph jammed her finger into the centre of his chest.

'Only a very little kidnap. Christo was desperate, wondering where his bride had disappeared to on their wedding day.'

'That's no excuse. She sent a message saying she was safe. Besides, you can't blame Emma for leaving when she discovered the real reason he'd married her.'

Slowly Damen shook his head. 'They've made their peace now. But that week Christo was mad with worry. I had to help him locate her. And you,' suddenly he leaned towards her, his free hand covering hers and capturing it against his chest, 'you knew where she was.'

'You *assumed* I did.' Steph kept her eyes on his face, rather than that broad chest where his heart thudded strongly beneath her palm.

'It was more than an assumption, Stephanie. It didn't take a genius to work out she'd had help disappearing so completely and quickly. I could see you were uncomfortable keeping quiet about Emma's whereabouts. I knew if I could just get you alone and persuade you...'

The heat in Steph's cheeks turned scorching hot, exploding in fiery darts that shot through her whole body. She ripped her hand from his grasp and stepped back.

'Is *that* what you call it? Persuasion?' Her breath came in sawing gasps that didn't fill her lungs.

Dull colour scored his sculpted cheekbones but Steph felt no satisfaction that she'd actually dented his ego or his conscience.

She was too busy remembering that it wasn't Damen but she who'd made the first move that night.

Exhausted from a long week at work, she'd had no excuse to refuse Damen when he arrived saying he had a lead on Emma's location. He'd asked her to go with him to persuade her back to her husband. Steph had known Emma was in Corfu, since she'd made Emma's travel arrangements. But she couldn't admit that. So she'd gone with Damen, only to doze off on the long drive out of the city.

When she'd woken the car had stopped and Damen was leaning towards her, his breath warm on her face. Half-awake and unthinking, she'd reacted instinctively and lifted her hand to his face. He'd stilled and Steph could have sworn the atmosphere turned electric with mutual need. Then his arms were around her and she was arching into him as he kissed her with a thoroughness that unravelled everything she thought she knew about desire, and every defence she'd ever erected.

Her hands had ploughed through that thick, soft hair with a desperation that betrayed an attraction she'd tried and failed to suppress. All week she'd seen Damen, hand-some, caring Damen, support his friend and Emma's family, checking on them all, leaving no stone unturned in the quest to find Emma.

It was only when they'd finally left the car for the deserted beach house that Steph discovered the truth. She'd been walking on air, her blood singing in her veins. Until Damen admitted why he'd brought her to that isolated place.

He'd hold her there till she told him where Emma was, for days if necessary. Even then she hadn't believed him. Thought he actually had a romantic rendezvous in mind. Till eventually she'd reached for her phone and he'd told her he'd taken it from her bag in the car and locked it away.

He hadn't been leaning towards her to wake her, or to steal a kiss. He'd been reaching into her handbag, palming her phone so she couldn't call for assistance.

And when she'd reached for him?

Well, why look a gift horse in the mouth? He must have decided that softening her up with a little seduction would make it easier to get to the truth.

Steph shut her eyes, trying to blot out the memory of that night. Of how she'd betrayed her yearning for a man who didn't care for her. Who'd callously used her attraction to him for his own ends. No doubt he'd silently laughed at her gullibility.

'Stephanie?' A firm hand gripped her elbow. 'Are you okay?'

'*Don't*. Touch. Me.'

One staggering step back and she came up against a cypress tree. Instead of sinking against it she stood straight and stared up into green eyes dark with concern.

He was a good actor. Last year in Australia she'd believed he was as attracted as she.

The worst of it was that to him it had merely been a *little* kidnap, since Christo had phoned soon after Damen's revelation with news he'd discovered Emma's whereabouts. Her abductor had then apologised for his 'drastic action' and driven her home, politely seeing her to her door in a painful parody of a date. All the time she'd squirmed at how she'd revealed her feelings for him. Feelings he didn't return. Feelings he'd callously used.

Steph had felt about an inch tall.

Like all those times when her dad had failed to show up, despite his promises. Because something had cropped up that was more important than spending time with his girl.

'I wanted to apologise.'

Damen's deep voice held a husky edge that might have sounded like guilt. Except Steph would rather trust a crocodile that claimed to be vegetarian than she would this man.

'You've done that before.'

Wide shoulders lifted. 'It obviously didn't work.'

'Work?' Her gaze slewed back to his face and she took in his serious expression.

'You haven't forgiven me.'

For a long time his eyes held hers, then she looked beyond him to the bluer than blue sky and the scented cypress trees. 'You can't have everything.'

She was *not* going to absolve his outrageous behaviour.

'Yet you haven't told Emma what happened.'

Unwillingly she turned back to him. 'Emma had enough to deal with. And later...' She shrugged. 'There was no reason to tell her. Especially as you're her husband's best friend. Why put her in the impossible position of disliking you when she'll have no choice but to see you regularly?'

'Is that how you feel? You dislike me?' Again that echo of something Steph couldn't identify in his tone.

Regret?

Probably more like curiosity. Steph was fairly certain most people approved of Damen Nicolaides, given his looks, charm and stonking great fortune.

She breathed deep, steadying herself. It was time to end this. 'I was brought up to be polite, Mr Nicolaides. But clearly you're too thick-skinned to get the message.' Steph wondered if anyone, particularly a woman, had ever said no to him. Had they all fallen victim to his charm? 'The answer is yes, I dislike you.'

To her chagrin he didn't react. Not even a flicker in that sharp green stare. Clearly her words had no impact on his monumental ego.

Her chin hiked higher. 'I'll be happy if I never have to see or speak with you again.'

That was when she saw it. A stiffening of muscles, drawing the skin tight across the hard planes of his face. A flare of imperious nostrils. A twitch of the lips. And those eyes…despite their cool colour they burned for a second with shocking heat.

A moment later Steph was left wondering if she'd imagined his reaction. He looked as he always did, effortlessly urbane and totally at ease, as if his only worry was deciding whether to summon his jet for a jaunt to Acapulco or Monte Carlo.

His mouth stretched into a smile that made Steph's thudding heart skip. It was a crying shame that the man should be so formidably attractive when he was such a louse.

'That's unfortunate. I was hoping to get to know you better. Spend some time together.'

'Together?' Steph couldn't believe it. Did he really think she'd be sucked into falling for his macho charisma again? Couldn't he comprehend how thoroughly she detested him? 'You have to be joking. I wouldn't spend time with you if you offered me a million dollars.'

A heartbeat's silence, a tic of pulse at his temple, just time enough for Steph to wonder how far her strident words had carried. She was turning towards the path back to the wedding when his voice halted her.

'Then how about two million dollars?'

CHAPTER TWO

THE WORDS WERE out before Damen could think about them. But even as they sank in, he felt a surge of satisfaction.

Because finally Stephanie looked at him with something other than disdain?

Or because instinct told him the offer, despite being instinctive, was pure genius?

He'd wanted a woman who was single, attractive, clever and short-term. Stephanie met his requirements exactly. The fact she didn't like him only made her more perfect.

Except for that niggle deep in Damen's belly when she looked at him like he was something unsavoury.

Then he felt guilt. Regret.

And, he admitted, indignation.

He knew he deserved her anger, understood he'd hurt her. But how could he have stood by and watched his best friend go crazy with worry, knowing Stephanie Logan held the answers he needed?

He'd tried everything he could think of to get the truth out of her but she'd withstood all his appeals for help. When those failed he'd acted decisively to end the farce that she didn't know where Emma was. His motives had been laudable. He'd done it for the best, to give Christo a chance to find his bride and sort out their problems.

Yet it was true Damen had been too taken up with getting answers to consider his actions from Stephanie's perspective. Until she'd looked at him with those huge brown eyes full of hurt. Even her subsequent lashing temper hadn't erased the memory of her embarrassment and pain. That night Damen felt emotions he hadn't felt in a decade or more. Since he'd faced his father that fateful night.

Damen had intended to see her again, to make things

right between them, except there'd been a business crisis that needed his personal attention and he'd had to leave.

Or maybe it was easier to walk away and not face what she made you feel.

'If that's your idea of a joke I don't appreciate it.'

Stephanie swung away, her loose, dark curls bouncing.

She'd had short hair in Melbourne. Short and severe, yet somehow the boyish style had emphasised the feminine allure of features that should be merely ordinary.

Watching those glossy curls swirl around her head, Damen recognised she was anything but ordinary. How could she be when she was so vibrant? The air around her crackled with energy and an inner force lit her features whether she was sad, happy or furious.

And when she kissed—

'It's no joke.'

That stopped her. She slammed to a stop and turned to face him. Her chin hiked up as if she had a chance of meeting his gaze on the same level. Yet, though she was far shorter, somehow she managed to look down that petite nose at him. One eyebrow arched and her velvety gaze turned piercing.

That was better.

Her anger he could handle. It was the shadow of hurt he'd seen before that discomfited him.

As if he, Damen Nicolaides, could be swayed by a tiny brunette's emotions! He regularly played hardball at the negotiating table with competitors, contractors, unions and regulators.

The idea was laughable. And yet...

'Obviously you're not serious. You'd never pay two million dollars to—'

'Spend time with you?' He stepped towards her, but cautiously, not wanting her to dash off in a temper before she heard him out. 'In fact I do mean it.'

She shook her head, her forehead wrinkling. 'How much have you had to drink?'

Damen felt his mouth stretch in a grin. 'Barely anything. I'm stone-cold sober.' Far from being insulted, he enjoyed her directness. Only his close family and Christo treated him like a real person these days. Most others were busy trying to get on his good side.

'It can't be a pick-up line because I know you have no interest in picking me up.'

Her voice was cool but the streaks of pink across her cheeks betrayed emotion. Instantly Damen was swept back to that night outside Melbourne. How delicious she'd been in his arms. How delectably flushed and aroused.

'So what's your game? Are you trying to make a fool of me again? Did you enjoy it so much you've developed a taste for it?'

She looked like she could spit fire, arms crossed, empty wine glass beating a tattoo against her bare arm. In her slinky green dress she looked like an angry sea sprite.

Damen felt a tug of desire. He had vivid recollections of how her initial, tentative caresses had grown demanding and surprisingly addictive.

He forced himself to concentrate.

'Come on, Stephanie. I'm not like that. You know why I did what I did.' Enough was enough. He'd inadvertently hurt her but she made him out to be some sort of sadistic manipulator. 'I've said I'm sorry. I'll do what I can to make amends for what I did.'

'Good.' She inclined her head regally. 'You can leave me alone. That will do nicely.'

With a flounce she spun away. The long dress flared out around her legs, drawing attention to her tiny waist. Damen's fingers twitched as he remembered the feel of her slim, restless body against his.

'Don't you want to hear about the two million dollars?' he said silkily, crossing his arms. One thing he knew. There were few people who'd spurn the chance to get their hands on that sort of money.

Naturally she paused. Money talked. Damen told himself he wasn't disappointed that she was like all the rest. He was pleased, because he needed her.

'I can't believe you're serious.'

'Oh, I'm serious.' He'd do whatever it took to bring peace to Clio and her family. Two million was nothing compared with their wellbeing.

'Okay, then.' Again that chin hitched high. Her eyes narrowed to suspicious slits. 'What do you want?'

'You.' He watched her stiffen and hurried on. 'Or, more precisely, your company in public.'

'In public?'

What had she thought? That he'd pay for her in his bed? His jaw tightened. He'd never paid for sex and he didn't intend to begin now. His voice was steely as he answered. 'Of course in public. This is a PR exercise, nothing else. I'm not proposing we become lovers.'

Inexplicably, though, his stomach clenched as her head jerked back and her cheeks turned pale.

As if he'd insulted her.

It reminded him of her bruised look that night in Australia after their kisses in the car. When she discovered he'd taken her there not for seduction but to demand the truth about Emma's location. He'd hurt her and clearly he wasn't forgiven.

The look in those liquid dark eyes when she'd woken to discover him leaning across her, slipping the phone from her bag, had been one of delight. Not surprise, but welcome. As if there was nothing more natural than the pair of them together.

For a few minutes Damen had forgotten why they were there and fallen under her sensual spell. It had been surprisingly potent and he'd been shocked at the depth of his response. The extent to which she distracted him from his purpose.

Ignoring a sharp pang that felt like guilt, Damen spoke. 'I need a woman to act as my companion, my girlfriend, for the next few months. And who'll keep the secret that it's a pretence. That's all.'

'That's all?' Her eyes rounded. 'What happened? You can't get a girlfriend? Have all the women in Greece finally seen past the smiles and the charm to the louse behind the mask?'

Now she tried his temper. A temper Damen was barely aware he had. For years everything in his world had gone the way he wanted it to. Except for the trying tendency of women to see him as a matrimonial prize.

Damen's chin lifted as he stood straighter. Stephanie's expression stilled, her eyes growing wary as she sensed his anger, yet she didn't retreat.

With enormous restraint Damen refused to take the bait. Stephanie's dislike of him meant she was perfect in this role. She'd never hanker for more from him than his money.

'We're not discussing my personal life, except to say that I don't have a lover at the moment. You wouldn't be stepping on anyone's toes.' She opened her mouth, no doubt to say something he didn't want to hear, so Damen kept talking. 'I need someone who can give the *appearance* of being my girlfriend.'

'Why?'

'Does it matter?'

'Of course it matters. No woman worth her salt would get involved in such a crazy scheme without knowing why. It sounds shonky. You're asking me to lie.'

'As I recall, it's not the first time you've done that.'

Her cheeks pinkened and despite his impatience Damen found himself intrigued as fire flashed in her eyes. He couldn't remember any other woman who telegraphed her

emotions that way, or who regularly managed to get a reaction from him.

'That was different! I was protecting my friend.'

'As I was protecting mine.'

Her breath exhaled in a slow stream as she clearly fought
for control.

'Okay, I'll bite, Mr Nicolaides. Tell me more.'

'Damen.' He stifled a sigh. He sensed he'd wait till Hades
froze before she willingly used his name. That should please
him, more proof that she had no scheme to become his girlfriend for real, yet he was chagrined. He wasn't used to
being summarily rejected by a woman. Especially a woman
who still...intrigued him.

He digested that. It could be a mistake, asking her to do
this when he wasn't totally immune to the appeal of those
big brown eyes or that trim figure.

Plus it would be problematic getting involved with Emma's best friend. He could do without the repercussions.

But if this scheme was to work he had to act now. Cassie's
wedding was soon and this masquerade had to seem plausible. The earlier reports filtered to the press and to Manos
that Damen had a live-in lover, the better. Anyone who
knew him would understand how momentous that was, for
in Damen's world the words 'live-in' and 'lover' never existed together.

'I want it to appear for the next month or two that I'm
committed to a woman.'

She shook her head, curls swirling around her face. 'But
why? As a decoy while you have an affair with a married
woman? Am I supposed to keep her husband off the scent?'
Her mouth pursed.

'No!' Where did she get these ideas? Did she think he
had no honour? 'I'd never touch another man's woman!'

Stephanie's expression didn't change. It was a new thing
to have his word doubted. Damen didn't like it.

He raked a hand through his hair, frustration rising.

'Someone has the idea, the completely wrong idea, that I'm planning to marry...a particular woman. I need a pretend lover to convince them they're wrong.'

'You led some poor female to believe you were serious about a relationship and now—'

'No!' Damen blinked as he realised his voice had risen to a roar.

He *never* shouted. Nor did he explain himself. His pride smarted and his chest felt tight with anger and frustration. Suddenly Stephanie Logan's suitability for this masquerade lessened. She had a knack for provoking him that no one else had.

'I haven't misled any woman. The woman in question has no interest in marrying me. It's her family that wants the marriage, primarily because of my fortune.'

'Now, that I can understand.'

Her tone implied no one would want Damen for himself, only for his money. That rankled. Especially as it cut too close to the truth.

The murky past raised its ugly head but he'd had years to practise avoiding painful memories. Ruthlessly he shoved thoughts of the past away.

And found his lips twitching.

A month with Stephanie Logan would whittle his ego down, that was for sure.

If he could get her to agree.

Had he ever met a woman so ready to think the worst of him?

'Listen, the woman and I are friends only. However, her father has other ideas and he's bullying her.'

'To marry you?'

Damen nodded. 'He's a determined man and he's making her life unbearable. He won't let it rest unless I show him my interests lie elsewhere.'

Did Stephanie's flush deepen or did he imagine it?

'So you *do* want camouflage.'

'Listen, Stephanie. No one will be hurt by this masquerade. On the contrary it will make life a whole lot easier for my friend and her family.'

For long moments Stephanie stared back at him. This time Damen found it impossible to read her thoughts. Was she leaning towards agreement? Wondering if she should ask for more money?

'No one would believe we were together.'

He frowned. 'Because we mix in different social circles?'

'You're saying you're out of my league?' She snapped out the words and he knew he'd offended her. 'Actually, my friends wouldn't believe it because I have better taste in men.'

Her bright eyes and angled chin signalled pure challenge. Strangely Damen found himself suppressing a smile. She was so determined to rile him. It made him wonder what it would be like if she put all that energy into something else. His thoughts strayed into scenarios that would make her blush if she knew.

'Why me?' she asked at last.

Damen shrugged. 'You're single. You've got some time free—Emma mentioned you were on holiday. And I know you wouldn't misinterpret this as a chance to establish yourself in my life permanently. The fact you dislike me is a point in your favour.'

Her eyes narrowed. 'Because any other woman would try to worm her way into your affections?'

He spread his hands wide. 'It's a possibility.'

She muttered something under her breath. The only word he heard was 'ego'.

Damen stiffened.

Did he truly want to tie himself for a couple of months to a woman who despised him? Would she even be able to play the part of besotted lover?

The answer was yes and yes.

Stephanie Logan was the ideal candidate for this masquerade. She was an outsider, unknown to friends or family in Greece. And he could trust her motives to be strictly short-term.

As for acting besotted…they said love was the opposite side of hate. Damen just had to harness all that emotional energy in a constructive direction. The way the atmosphere sparked and sizzled when they were together would convince even a sceptic that they were connected.

'And you don't want to settle down because you're busy being a carefree bachelor?' Her voice dripped disapproval.

'Something like that.'

Damen had no intention of explaining his plan to avoid marriage. He'd never have kids. Eventually he'd pass the family enterprise to his sisters' children. Damen had enough family without creating more. Especially as he'd always wonder if his wife had married him for himself or his money.

'I still don't understand why you asked me and not someone else, but the answer's no. I don't like deception and you're the last man I want to spend time with.'

Damen stared at Stephanie's flushed face, her clenched jaw and those high breasts rising and falling with each rapid breath.

He wanted to seal this deal here and now but he read the warning signs. Stephanie was a passionate woman in a temper, ready to lash out, even if it meant passing up an opportunity she'd later regret.

She needed time to consider the advantages of his proposition.

He had a little time. She was staying at the villa while Emma and Christo went on their honeymoon. And his yacht was moored offshore.

'Don't decide now, Stephanie. I'll come back for your final answer later.' Then, scooping the empty glass dangling from her hand, he strolled back to the party.

* * *

Take your time!

Because the man couldn't accept a simple no! He was so arrogant, so stupendously sure of himself, he made Steph's blood boil.

Thinking about Damen made her pulse skitter and her breath came in hard, short bursts. She remembered him saying she was perfect for his plan because she wouldn't try to worm her way into his affections.

As if!

There was only one worm here and it wasn't her.

But, she remembered as she leaned back on the padded sunlounger by the pool, he wasn't here, was he?

Typical of him to throw out such an outrageous proposition then not follow through. Obviously he was toying with her. She'd known he couldn't be serious. Even a shipping tycoon didn't squander two million dollars on such a farcical scheme.

He made her so *angry*. Angry enough to tell him to his face she had better taste in men than to stoop to him. There was a laugh. Her taste in men was abysmal. Nor had there really been men in her life, not the way he'd think.

Steph hadn't seen Damen Nicolaides since last night when they and the other wedding guests waved farewell to the newlyweds.

From things Emma had let drop Steph suspected they were on their way to Iceland to see the Northern Lights. It was a place Steph longed to visit but now, like all those other places on her travel list, it was out of her reach. She'd make the most of these days on Corfu. It was likely to be her last holiday.

Steph picked up her pen and focused on her list of potential employers, but her heart wasn't in it. She'd already contacted the best agencies and there was no work.

Even when she got a new job, her troubles wouldn't be over. There was the matter of all the money she had to recoup. The wheels of justice turned slowly. By the time the authorities caught Jared, if they ever did, her money would have disappeared. And Gran's too.

Steph's belly clenched as she thought of Gran, so eager to support her only granddaughter's first business venture that she'd put her life savings into it.

If Steph had known, she wouldn't have let her take the risk. She'd never have introduced her to Jared.

Steph shook her head. If-onlys were pointless. Jared, her one-time boss and almost business partner, had skipped the country, leaving Steph with nothing but a debt she couldn't service. And Gran with no way of funding the move to the retirement village she'd planned.

Steph ground her teeth and flung the notebook down.

A steady wage wouldn't rectify her financial problems. It was lucky she'd paid for her return flight to Australia months ago. She had barely enough for a week's rent in a hostel when she got back.

There was one obvious way out of her troubles.

Tell Emma. Her friend and her husband were wealthy. Emma wouldn't hesitate to help.

But the thought sickened Steph. She couldn't leech off Emma. This was *her* mistake. *She* had to fix it. She'd trusted Jared, believed him when he said he was moving the money to put a deposit on their new premises.

Besides, money issues could destroy friendships. Emma and Steph had been best mates since they started high school, when Steph had championed quiet Emma and in return been gifted with the truest friend she'd ever made. She'd never jeopardise that.

Nausea rose as she remembered earlier days when she'd still lived with her mother. Suddenly the kids next door weren't allowed to visit. They'd shunned her. Ugly words had been hurled and a shame she'd been too young to under-stand weighed her down. Because Steph's mother, battling to support them both on her cleaner's wage, had borrowed from her friend next door. Borrowed money she couldn't repay. The friendship died and they'd had to move again to a smaller flat.

Steph's mother had worked hard but she'd never been able to hold on to money. They'd lived from hand to mouth until Steph had finally been packed off to live with Gran.

Steph grimaced. She'd been determined not to be like her mother. From the day she got her first paper round then worked several part-time jobs, she'd scrimped to save and contribute to Gran's housekeeping.

So proud of herself, she'd been. Confident about this exciting venture with Jared, a bespoke travel company, catering to those who wanted an individualised holiday experience.

It had all turned to dust.

Steph swung off the lounger and shot to her feet. She needed a plan. A way to salvage Gran's savings at least.

A way to get money quickly, not in twenty years.

Two million dollars.

The tantalising echo of that deep voice rippled through her. Damen made his crazy proposition sound almost reasonable.

With two million dollars she could buy Gran a home in the retirement village she had her eye on, with the lake view. There'd be money to start again. To avoid the trap her mother had fallen into, working low-paid jobs to get by.

Steph had loved her mother but vowed to learn from her mistakes. She'd be financially independent and never be taken in by a guy who'd let her down. Like Steph's feckless father, who'd never provided emotional or financial support and then disappeared for ever.

A bitter laugh clogged Steph's throat. Look at her now!

She'd fallen for the double whammy. Jared hadn't romanced her, but she'd believed his plausible talk about a new venture, put her money into it, and lost everything.

It was enough to make a woman crazy. She strode towards the beach path. She needed to work off this agitation then find a solution.

She turned the corner at the end of the villa and walked into a wall that shouldn't be there.

A wall a few inches over six feet tall, cushioned with muscle and smelling of the outdoors and hot male flesh.

Steph's middle turned inside out and a fluttering rose in her chest.

'Stephanie. I'd hoped to find you.'

His smile, a flash of perfect white teeth against olive-gold skin should have made her wonder how much Damen had spent on dental surgery. But she suspected it was all real. Just as every inch of that tall frame was the real deal, lean yet strongly muscled. Wearing cut-offs and a T-shirt that clung to that impressive chest, it was clear his masculine appearance owed nothing to his tailor.

Steph swallowed annoyance. Was anything about the man, apart from his morals, less than perfect?

Damen looked into those sparkling eyes and felt a punch to the solar plexus. Stronger even than yesterday, when the sight of Stephanie, alluring in her long gown, had dried his mouth. Only for a moment, because no woman had the power to unnerve him. He wouldn't allow it.

Yesterday it had been due to surprise. Stephanie had seemed so different with those dusky, clustering curls and formal dress. She'd been ultra-feminine and disturbingly sultry.

And today?

His hands closed on her bare arms as he took her in. The scarlet one-piece swimsuit should have looked demure, but on Stephanie's slender curves…

Damen yanked his gaze to her face. That was when he read something other than the scorn he'd seen yesterday.

Was that distress as well as anger?

He looked past her, searching for the person who'd upset

her, but there was no one. Beneath his hold she was taut, almost vibrating, like a wire strung too tight.

'What's wrong?'

'Nothing's wrong.' Predictably her chin rose and she drew a deep breath that tested Damen's determination not to ogle her trim body. 'Except you've intruded on my privacy.'

It felt like relief to have her snark at him, yet Damen wasn't convinced. There were shadows around her eyes, shadows he hadn't put there. She'd already been upset when she stormed towards him.

Bizarre to feel protective of a woman who despised him, yet...

He released his hold, surprised when, for a millisecond, she swayed towards him. Then she planted her feet as if to steady herself.

'I've come for an answer.' Damen folded his arms over his chest, surprised to discover his heart thudding fast.

'You were serious?'

He held her gaze. 'Absolutely. Two million dollars for a couple of months of your time.'

She swallowed and Damen repressed the impulse to lean closer, pushing his advantage.

'Think of all you could do with the money.' He was surprised she'd delayed. Any other woman would have leapt at the chance straight away.

Stephanie Logan had a contrary streak.

Surprising that didn't deter him.

Her eyelids flickered, veiling her eyes as she gnawed lips he knew to be soft and delicious. He was so focused on her mouth it took a moment to realise she'd turned that bright gaze on him again.

'Okay, you've got a deal. I'll be your fake girlfriend for two million dollars.'

CHAPTER THREE

TRIUMPH WAS A surge of adrenalin in Damen's arteries. A lifting of tension he hadn't been aware of till the weight across his shoulders eased.

Because the way was clear to scotch Manos's wedding expectations.

Because Damen hated the idea of people he cared for, like Clio and her mother, being hurt. Especially when it was his fault.

His thoughts strayed to that terrible time when he'd been the catalyst for the disaster that rocked his family. He yanked his mind from that and back on track.

Stephanie at his side, sexy, provoking, intriguing... Which of course was only important as it made her the perfect person to play his pretend lover.

Damen's thoughts slowed on the word 'lover'. Slowed and circled. Despite her animosity and her insults, she intrigued him as no woman had in years.

Another reason to remember this was purely business.

'But I have conditions.'

'Conditions?' He frowned. Was she going to try to negotiate for more money? She must guess he was desperate or he'd never have made the offer.

'Yes.' She folded her arms and her breasts burgeoned against the top of her swimsuit. Damen breathed deep and concentrated on her face. He refused to be distracted during negotiations. 'I want everything spelled out in a legal contract.'

He released his breath. 'Is that all?' Of course there'd be a contract, including a watertight non-disclosure clause so she couldn't sell her story or details of his life to the press.

'Not all.' She paused. 'I want half the money in advance when I sign.'

Damen saw colour rise up her chest and throat into her cheeks. She swallowed quickly and the pulse at the base of her neck beat a rapid tattoo. She expected an argument. Obviously it was important that she get the funds quickly.

Why? Was she in financial difficulty? Or couldn't she wait to get spending?

Damen was on the verge of asking but stopped himself. He didn't need to know her motivations, despite the urgent curiosity he refused to give in to. This was a deal. Her services for his money.

'Done.'

Her eyes widened and he fancied he read surprise there. And nerves. Why? Because she'd hoped he wouldn't agree? Was the offer of two million so alluring she'd been persuaded despite her better judgement?

Now he was being fanciful.

'One other thing.' Her gaze settled near his ear.

Now he was definitely intrigued. Despite the disparity between them, in wealth, power and physical size, Stephanie always met his gaze.

This condition she'd left till last was vitally important.

'No kissing.'

Finally her eyes locked on his and a sizzle pierced Damen's belly, driving down like a hammering pile driver. Then the connection was severed and she stared at his ear again.

'Sorry?'

'You heard me.' She dropped her arms to her sides then almost immediately refolded them. 'I'll play your girlfriend in public, but I won't kiss you, *and*,' she hurried on as if expecting him to interrupt, 'I won't have you kissing me. No lip locks. I want that spelled out in the contract.'

Damen lifted an eyebrow, intrigued. 'If we're lovers people will expect us to be intimate and show affection.'

Her flush intensified. Damen's curiosity deepened. Was she annoyed or embarrassed?

'Intimate in private. In public there are ways of showing affection without kissing.'

Damen shoved his hands into his pockets. 'I'm paying you an enormous sum. I expect you to be completely convincing.'

'And I will be. I just won't kiss you.'

'For religious reasons? Health reasons? I can assure you you're not going to catch some terrible illness.'

She unlocked tightly crossed arms and spread her hands. 'Because I don't care to, okay? Once was more than enough. I won't repeat that mistake.'

Damen was about to say it hadn't felt like a mistake. In fact their kiss had moved him in ways he wasn't used to.

That in itself was reason enough not to say it.

He frowned. 'Then how do you intend to persuade people we're lovers?'

She made a vague gesture. 'By hanging on your every word. Looking into your eyes. Snuggling up—'

'Snuggling? So we're allowed to touch?'

Stephanie's mouth thinned and Damen suspected she stifled the urge to swear.

'Don't be asinine. Sarcasm doesn't suit you.' She shook her head and those lush curls brushed her cheeks. 'There are ways of signalling attraction and intimacy without—'

'Putting my lips on yours.' He watched her blink and something inside him shifted.

Did this woman have any idea how provocative, how downright dangerous, it was to throw down an ultimatum like that? Especially to the man paying such a price for her company?

It was more than an ultimatum. It was a challenge.

Damen didn't back down from challenges. He won them.

'Prove you can be convincing as my lover or the deal is off.'

Damen saw dismay flicker in that bright gaze. Was she going to renege?

Disappointment stirred.

He'd imagined, after the way Stephanie Logan had once stood up for her friend Emma, defying both him and Christo to keep her secret, and the way she'd lambasted him after he'd abducted her, that nothing could daunt this woman. Now he read something in her expression that made him doubt. Maybe he'd misjudged—

She stepped towards him, so close he caught the scent of sun lotion and vanilla. That vanilla fragrance stirred memories of her in his arms, kissing him with a fervour that shredded his control.

Damen was still grappling with that when a small, firm hand closed around his bare forearm, curling loosely yet seeming to brand him. A shiver of something disturbingly like delight reverberated through him.

Stephanie leaned in, her eyes a golden brown that for a change looked soft and melting rather than distrustful.

He liked that look. Very much.

Just as he liked the way her lips parted as if being close to him affected her breathing.

Damen realised his own lungs were working harder. In anticipation, he told himself. If she couldn't convince as his girlfriend he'd have to find someone else.

He didn't want anyone else.

The unsettling notion stirred then was squashed as Stephanie moved nearer.

Sweetly rounded breasts jiggled a hair's breadth from his arm as she rose on tiptoe. She was so close he felt her warm breath on his face. It should have been a mere waft of air. It felt like a deliberate, sensuous stroke of her fingers. Her lips formed a pout that turned her mouth into an invitation to kiss.

Damen didn't bend his head. He stood, waiting.

He didn't have to wait long. She planted her other hand

on his chest, over the spot where his heart accelerated to a quicker beat. Her fingers splayed, slid across the contours of muscle, then stopped.

She blinked and he had the impression she was as surprised by that caress as he was.

Damen expected her to pull away but she leaned still nearer. Delight surged as those brown eyes locked on his in clear invitation.

'Damen,' she murmured in a throaty voice that belonged in the bedroom. Her fingers walked up his chest. Soft fingertips flirted against his collarbone and his flesh tightened.

Something jolted through him. Delight? Anticipation? Both?

He reminded himself this was a game, a test. It wasn't real. But his body ignored logic. Heat trailed low in his groin.

Stephanie leaned still closer, her full breast warm and intoxicatingly inviting against his arm.

'You have no idea,' she whispered, so close that they breathed the same air, 'how very, very alluring I find...'

Damen inclined his head, drawn to those luminous eyes fringed with lush dark lashes. And more, by the conviction she'd finally put aside her dislike, giving in to the attraction that had connected them from the first.

Her fingers on his lips stopped him just as he heard '... your two million dollars.'

Abruptly she was gone.

Damen chilled. It felt like she'd cut him off at the knees.

He'd issued the challenge. He should have known Stephanie Logan would accept it and shouldn't have let himself get distracted. She wasn't the sort to back down.

Or, apparently, to give up the chance of a couple of million.

His lips twisted. He needed to remember that. No matter how sweet he'd once found her. How he'd respected her loyalty to her friend even as he'd cursed her obstinacy.

She was doing this for money and far more convincingly than he'd thought possible.

An undercurrent of doubt channelled through his belly. His hackles rose.

She'd only done what he'd demanded, prove she could play the convincing lover. Yet, looking into that pretty face flushed with satisfaction, he was irresistibly reminded of another woman who'd been all too convincing at feigning ardour and even love.

A woman who'd almost wrecked his life and who'd been the catalyst for his greatest regret.

'How'd I do?' Stephanie stuck her hands on her hips, looking up expectantly.

Did she expect applause?

Grudgingly Damen realised she probably deserved it. She didn't care for him but he'd insisted on a demonstration of fake affection. It was unreasonable to feel betrayed by how well she'd pretended.

'Well enough.'

She frowned but Damen wasn't going to heap praise on her ability to lie.

The muffled voice of his conscience said he was unreasonable. He'd be lying about this fake relationship too. At least Stephanie was upfront about her motives.

Yet it took an effort to shake off his dissatisfaction as he looked into her features, again wearing that familiar, guarded expression.

'So we have a deal?'

'I'll have the contract drawn up straight away. With the specifications you requested.'

Half the money in advance. And no kissing.

Maybe it was his unsettled mood. Maybe it was annoyance at how she'd dredged up negative memories. More probably it was the way she'd bruised his pride, being immune to him when just months ago she'd been eager for his touch.

Whatever the reason, Damen found himself adding a mental corollary to their deal. He'd stick to their bargain but he'd make Stephanie Logan regret her no-kissing rule. In fact, he'd make it his business to ensure she too felt this tingling dissatisfaction that their affair wasn't real.

He'd seduce her into wanting him again.

You're crazy. You hate deception. Yet you're going to lie for a man you don't even like.

Steph threaded her fingers together, willing the voice in her head to stop.

It's worse than that. You don't like him but you're still attracted, aren't you?

'Stephanie?'

'Sorry.' She turned her gaze back to the tall man whose presence filled the study of Emma's villa. Sunlight streamed through the windows, slanting across those high-cut cheekbones before pooling on the papers he'd brought.

'I said, I had the contract drawn up in English, so you don't need a translator.'

'Thank you.' Surprised at his thoughtfulness, she smiled, despite her nerves.

She should have guessed Damen would think of that. He was thorough. In Melbourne he'd been a pillar of strength for his friend, leaving no stone unturned to locate Christo's missing bride. Damen seemed to think of everything.

Suppressing a shiver, Steph crossed to the desk on reluctant feet. Now it came to the crunch she had doubts.

Except Damen would transfer cash to her account the moment she signed. Cash she'd use to buy a lovely, purpose-built home for her grandmother in the development she had her heart set on.

How could she refuse?

Yet her movements were slow as she took the chair he held out. The contract sat before her, a stylish fountain pen beside it.

She breathed deep but instead of settling her nerves, it had the opposite effect. For she inhaled an attractive woodsy scent that she identified as Damen's. Rich, warm and far too appealing.

Steph shut her eyes and suddenly she was back in the garden yesterday, when Damen had threatened to scrap this deal unless she could play the convincing lover.

She'd felt challenged, daunted and a little too excited at being up against all that magnificent manliness. Her heart had raced and she'd told herself it was because she refused to back down. The prize was too big.

Steph had felt a surge of recklessness and been buoyed up by it. It was a welcome change after so much recent self-blame and doubt. For a few moments she'd felt her old self, confident, decisive and practical. Able to handle anything. Sheer relief at that once familiar feeling of assurance had filled her.

Until she'd closed the gap between them to kissing distance. Then she'd felt like a mouse who'd unwittingly been lured between a cat's paws. The heat in Damen's eyes had slammed into her and she realised she played with fire.

She'd retreated from him and suddenly, it seemed, she'd been wrong. There was no fire in his eyes. No desire. Damen Nicolaides didn't want her. He'd never wanted her.

He'd made that embarrassingly clear in Melbourne.

She'd been relieved at the reminder. Truly relieved.

What she'd seen flash in those stunning eyes was pique. Anger that she could act the part so easily yet remain immune to him.

Well, not immune, but she'd do whatever it took to hide that from him!

'Have you finished reading?' His deep voice came from over her shoulder and her eyes popped open.

'I like to take my time with legal documents.'

Not that that had stopped Jared running off with her money. Cold settled in Steph's bones and she set her teeth.

This deal seemed the only way to recoup what she'd lost, not just the money but her control over her life.

Yet she couldn't ignore the feeling it was a mistake.

But she needed to take the risk to reverse the plight she'd put herself and her beloved Gran in. Playing safe wouldn't help now.

Even if it didn't feel safe, she wouldn't fall for Damen Nicolaides again. She was over him, or almost over him. A few weeks in his company would destroy any lingering weakness. He didn't want her, so what was the risk?

Steph concentrated on the contract, reading each sentence carefully, grateful it was set out in simple terms. Her eyes rounded at the penalties she'd incur if she sold her story, but as she had no intention of broadcasting her time with Damen, that was no problem. She had to decide what to tell Emma, but that could wait.

Her breath eased out. There it was, the payment. Half today and half in eight weeks.

And there was her other stipulation.

No kiss on the lips unless specifically verbally invited by Ms Logan.

What an ego this guy had! As if she'd *ever* invite him to kiss her.

Steph frowned. No kiss on the lips. Surely she'd stipulated no kissing at all? Then she recalled saying 'No lip locks'. She reached for the pen. Should she change it?

'Is there a problem?'

She looked up to see Damen, hands in his trouser pockets, wearing a bland expression she suspected hid boredom. There was nothing in his expression that hinted at attraction. All he cared about was convincing people he had a new lover. It was a business deal, nothing else.

Why quibble over terminology? Over a kiss on the lips as opposed to any kiss? Damen wasn't interested in her kisses.

With a determined smile Steph picked up the pen and signed the contract.

'Excellent.' Damen nodded and drew out his phone. 'I'll organise the transfer of funds.'

See? It was easy and straightforward.

Soon Gran would have the home she wanted and a comfortable nest egg too, and Steph would be free of debt.

So why did her neck tingle with a premonition that this wouldn't be safe or easy after all?

CHAPTER FOUR

DAMEN STEPPED ONTO the main deck of his yacht and paused. He'd searched for Stephanie through half the vessel till a crew member mentioned she was outside. Now he saw her, barefoot and compellingly attractive in cut-off white jeans and a red-and-white-striped top.

Usually his girlfriends wore designer labels and regularly checked their hair and make-up. Stephanie didn't bother with make-up and her clothes didn't come from exclusive boutiques. Yet too often he found himself watching her, unable to look away.

He couldn't put his finger on why she drew him. She was attractive rather than beautiful. Engaging. Appealing.

She leaned out, drinking in the view as they came into Athens, curls lifting in the breeze and every line of her body straining forward in excitement. A smile lit her face.

A smile she rarely turned on him.

A now familiar sensation stirred. It was a mix of appreciation, anticipation and annoyance. Though he'd given her time, choosing to sail rather than fly from Corfu to the capital, she was still guarded around him.

That wouldn't do if Manos was to believe they were lovers.

Besides, her cool distance rankled. He was used to fending off women, not exerting himself to draw them closer.

Maybe Stephanie Logan was good for him. Clio always said he had it easy with women.

Not this woman.

At least she wasn't trying to engage his interest, as so many other women had. Yet there had to be a happy medium.

There'd been a couple of memorable times when her defences had tumbled. Like when they'd stopped off the island of Kefalonia for some snorkelling and a sea turtle had swum by. Stephanie had been so delighted she'd grabbed Damen's arm, her face wreathed in smiles.

For the rest of that sojourn he'd basked in her warmth and enthusiasm, enjoying the camaraderie and, he admitted, her approval as he shared his knowledge about the species and efforts being made to protect them.

That was the way she needed to be with him if they were to seem like lovers. No more tiptoeing around each other.

Damen had given her time. He'd waited long enough.

He stepped into the sunshine and felt a fillip of anticipation as Stephanie swung towards him. As if she was as attuned to his presence as he was to hers.

Her eyes ate him up and answering arousal kick-started in his belly. Then, as usual, her expression smoothed out, turning bland. But Damen focused on that moment of unguarded awareness. Despite her disapproval there was still attraction.

That was what they needed to persuade Manos. Damen intended to tap into it, starting now.

'*Kopela mou!* There you are.' He strolled to her side and wrapped his arm around her, drawing her close.

Stephanie froze, her head swinging up. 'What are you doing?' Her whisper was fierce.

'Beginning our liaison, sweetheart. What else?' He settled his hand on her hip and bent closer, enjoying her little shiver of response. He'd been right. For all her disapproval, Stephanie felt this attraction too. His mouth curved in a lazy smile. 'We're in Athens, or almost, and any one of those vessels you're watching could have curious eyes turned this way.'

His gesture encompassed the traffic in and out of the busy port. 'The *Amphitrite* is well known and there's money in selling photos of an elusive billionaire and his new lover.'

'Photos?' Her eyes widened as she turned to stare at the

harbour. 'You mean the paparazzi keep you under surveil-
lance?' Her voice sounded brittle with shock.

Had he just destroyed an innocent's illusions? But it was
better she was prepared for the inevitable media specula-
tion. An unknown Australian, appearing at his side out of
nowhere, would provoke interest.

Was that why he'd been so determined it should be Stephanie at his side? To get maximum coverage for this masquerade?

It was convenient to think so but Damen knew his motives were more complex. More personal.

'There's nothing to be scared of. I'll protect you. They
won't invade our privacy.' Or they'd suffer the consequences. 'Especially if we provide some photo opportunities.'

He turned, curling his index finger under her chin and
lifting her face towards his.

To her credit she didn't shy away, but nor did she look
lover-like. If there was a photographer out there with a tele-
photo lens they would see his companion wary rather than
enthusiastic. He needed to remedy that, quickly.

Steph told herself there was nothing to be nervous about in
broad daylight on the open sea. Except the idea of hidden
cameras trained on them sent tension darting through her.
Plus Damen's expression did little to reassure.

He barely touched her, yet the warmth of the skin-to-skin
touch felt intimate. It was a lover's caress.

No other man had touched her like this.

There'd been no lovers. Her early experiences, with a
stressed, distracted mother and an absent father who never
kept his promises had made her wary of emotional intimacy.
And from her teens on she'd put in long hours working while
her peers partied. The closest she'd come to letting down
her guard and giving in to passion had been with Damen
Nicolaides.

How he'd gloat if he knew! It would feed his already enormous ego.

'What are you doing?' Was that reedy voice hers?

'Providing a photo opportunity.' His mouth kicked up at one side, driving a groove down his cheek that was ridiculously sexy. Or maybe it was his intense stare that was sexy, as if he was aware of nothing but her.

Steph breathed out slowly, finding calm. The notion of Damen unaware of anything but her was laughable. This was an act for the benefit of the public. The realisation eased her racing pulse.

'You really think there are paparazzi out there?'

He shrugged. 'Probably. It pays to be careful. From now on it's best we act in character.'

In character.

As lovers, he means.

Steph gulped and told herself she could do this. She had to. She'd accepted a great wad of his money and it was currently being used to purchase Gran's new home.

Yet now it came to the crunch, with his body a mere hand span away and his breath feathering her face, the warning voice Steph had ignored for days became strident.

'What is it, Stephanie?' Damen actually sounded concerned, which made her wonder what he read in her face.

She tried to smooth her expression. 'This is tougher than I expected.'

Because in his embrace she felt things she'd vowed she wouldn't. Even knowing this was a charade, it was hard not to respond to the evocative tenderness of his touch and the hint of blatant possessiveness.

That scared her. Steph didn't want to be possessed by any man. She was her own woman. She'd learned never to be reliant and had no intention of forgetting that lesson, especially after the way Damen had made a fool of her.

'You've got cold feet?' His fingers tightened on her waist

and a crease was carved between those ebony eyebrows. 'It's too late. You signed a contract.'

His voice was terse, at odds with the lingering hint of a smile.

The disparity chilled her, sending a shiver scudding down her backbone. It was proof that appearances and embraces could lie. They had before with this man.

'Of course I've got cold feet. I'm not used to living a lie. But,' she said when he opened his mouth, 'I won't go back on my word.'

Especially since she no longer had the money he'd paid her.

'I knew I could count on you.' His voice dropped a notch, burring like rough suede across her bare neck and arms.

That, too, was a lie. That hint of desire in his voice. Yet some fatally feminine part of her responded, secretly thrilled.

Steph swallowed.

She was in trouble. Deep trouble.

But there was no escape.

His face tilted and his hand glided along to her jaw, her cheek, brushing her unruly hair back. She'd been too busy before she came to Greece and a hairdresser had been an unnecessary expense. She wished she'd had her hair cut short again, as strong fingers tunnelled through her curls, massaging her scalp in delicious circles that loosened her tense shoulders.

Her blood thickened and slowed and she found herself leaning into his touch.

Not to convince unseen eyes that they were lovers, but because Damen's touch was magic. Slow, sure and sensual, it mocked her determination to keep her distance.

He'd done this before, pretended attraction when there was none, yet even pride couldn't make her pull away.

If she did he'd realise his touch bothered her.

She was caught whatever she did.

Steph opened her mouth to say something, anything to divert him into conversation, when that arm at her waist tightened and his head lowered.

For a second shock held her still, then her hands went to his broad chest, flat against hot muscle and thin cotton as she tried to hold him at a distance.

She needn't have worried. He stopped a scant centimetre away, but his mouth was at her temple, lips scraping her skin as he spoke.

'Try not to look fazed. We're supposed to be lovers, remember?'

How could she forget?

With an effort that felt shockingly like no effort at all, Steph made her hands slide up his chest. Of their own volition they continued, curling around his neck. It felt hard and strong, the flesh there smooth and warm.

It was like the day he'd insisted she prove she could act the part of his lover. She'd made the first move, pleased with her boldness, until proximity to Damen made her body go soft and eager. As if it had been waiting to get close to him.

'Much better,' he purred against her forehead and to Steph's dismay she felt the words like an unfurling ribbon that trailed down through her body.

'You're not supposed to kiss me,' she protested, far too aware of the graze of his mouth.

The protest sounded limp, but she needed words to keep him at a distance when her body refused to obey her command not to melt against him.

'Hardly a kiss, *kopela mou*.' A pause and then he spoke again, his voice deeper than before. 'You'd know it if I kissed you.'

She would indeed. She had perfect recall of the last time. Of how she'd thrown caution to the wind as their mouths fused and desire had quaked through her.

It had been wonderful and cataclysmic at the same time, leaving the defences she'd spent a lifetime constructing in ruins.

'Not that I will, of course, given our contract.' He paused. 'Not without a specific, spoken invitation.'

Steph licked her lips. She was about to blurt out that she'd never give such an invitation, when instinct stopped the words. It would sound like a challenge and the last thing she needed was to provoke Damen Nicolaides into seeing this as a game of one-upmanship.

'How long do we have to stay like this?'

She hitched a breath, conscious of his torso so close she could almost feel it abrading her budding nipples. Heat drenched her. She told herself it was a hot day and Damen held her too close. But Steph wasn't that innocent. This heat came from deep inside. From the feminine core that gloried in being held by Damen. The part of her that had sprung to life once before in his arms.

That untamed, unthinking woman terrified her. She couldn't let her loose. She had to keep control.

'You make this sound like a chore, Stephanie.' Once more his voice drifted low on her name to a note that settled in her bones.

Steph drew a deep breath then stilled when it brought her breasts into contact with Damen. Did she imagine a change in the tempo of his breath tickling her forehead? A tightening in the clasp of that hand at her waist?

She didn't have time to be sure, for Damen stepped back, just enough to watch her with enigmatic eyes. For a moment she felt as if she were sinking out of her depth. Then his mouth crooked up in that slight smile she was coming to know and enjoy far too much.

'But practice makes perfect and in Athens we'll get plenty of practice.'

'We will?' Steph rubbed her palms together, trying to erase the tingling memory of his flesh against hers.

'Of course. I have business here but we'll go out too. Plenty of opportunities to be seen together.'

It was a timely reminder that this was for show. The closeness, his touch, the way his gaze lingered.

'Will she be in Athens? The woman you were involved with?'

That cleared her head like a shower of ice water. The thought of the woman who was the reason for this charade. No matter what Damen said, she was clearly important to him.

Steph reserved judgement on whether the mystery woman was really just Damen's friend or, more likely, his lover. Yet she felt something akin to dislike for the unknown woman.

Because Damen cared so much for her that he'd embark on this outrageous scheme?

It couldn't be that. Steph wasn't *jealous*.

'That needn't concern you.' His hand dropped and the remnants of that satisfied smile disintegrated.

So she was in Athens. Would Steph meet her? Would she even know her if she did?

She folded her arms and looked straight back at that narrowed green stare.

'This masquerade won't work if you're secretly meeting a lover on the side. Someone's bound to find out—'

Damen shook his head and said something sharp in Greek. Steph didn't need to understand the language to hear scorn and impatience.

'How many times do I have to tell you she's not my lover? I don't have a lover!' His voice rose as he made a dismissive gesture. 'The only girlfriend I have is you, Stephanie.'

This was the second time she'd provoked an unguarded response from Damen. Steph told herself she shouldn't be pleased at puncturing his formidable self-assurance. At seeing emotion flare in those heavy-lidded eyes. Yet she was.

The sight made her feel less helpless, less a mere pawn caught in his machinations.

'Careful, Damen.' She wagged her finger. 'If there are paparazzi out there, they'll see you scowling at me. That would destroy the illusion you care about me before we start.'

Even if he did look dramatically sexy with those dark eyebrows scrunched and that strong jaw honed tight.

For a second he didn't react. Then Damen surprised her with a crack of laughter, his face creasing into a smile of rueful amusement that tugged at something deep inside her.

'What they'll think is that we've had a spat. But that's okay because it gives us the chance to make up, very publicly.'

His eyes danced and anticipation swirled through her at the thought of making up with Damen.

Till she realised what she was doing and slammed a brake on her thoughts.

She'd assumed a few days on his yacht would cement her dislike but her feelings for Damen were ambiguous. He got to her in a way no other man did. Even the way he insisted on using her full name, lingering on the syllables as if savouring them, unravelled her defences.

Steph leaned on the railing, needing to look at something other than this man who disturbed her so easily. She saw a marina filled with luxury yachts. Some almost as enormous and beautiful as the *Amphitrite*. Maybe there was some billionaire's convention in town.

'Are we staying on the yacht?'

Not that 'yacht' seemed the right word for a ship with its own helipad, cinema, glass-bottomed pool and umpteen guest suites.

Steph had been in awe, until Damen's insistence that she was free to use anything she wanted, and the genuine friendliness of the staff, put her at ease. She'd earmarked a cosy corner of the library as her own and grown used to the state-of-the-art gym equipment. Playing the doting girlfriend would be easier if she could retreat to her comfortable stateroom.

'No, we'll head to my apartment.'

'Just an apartment?' She turned to look at him as he joined her at the railing, trying to hide her nerves. Suddenly this masquerade felt uncomfortably real. 'You surprise me. I thought you'd have a posh town house.'

Actually, she hadn't thought about it. The opulence of his superyacht had been a revelation. She'd known Damen was rich, but this level of wealth was far beyond her experience.

'Sorry to disappoint.' The curve of his mouth told her that her jab didn't bother him. 'But in Athens I find an apartment convenient. I'm sure you'll find it comfortable.'

'I'm sure I will.' If his yacht was any indication it would be gorgeous and purpose built. He probably owned the rest of the building too.

'And it's convenient for shopping. I've had a list drawn up of the boutiques that might be best for you.'

'That's kind.' If a little strange. 'But I doubt I'll be shopping.'

If she had time in Athens she intended to use it to see the sights she'd read about. Besides, the money she'd got from Damen had already been sent to Australia for Gran and to put towards the business debt Jared had left her with. The business loan still needed servicing even though there was now no business.

Damen's eyebrows lifted. 'You'll need new clothes.'

Steph straightened, pushing her shoulders back. Her hackles rose. 'Are you saying I don't measure up to your exalted standards?'

Damen read the flash of heat in those wide brown eyes and felt a frisson of awareness.

It was like that each time he and Stephanie argued. Or touched.

Her pride and contrariness were a nuisance. Yet he relished each clash, revelled in the moments when Stephanie shared her feelings and thoughts instead of keeping her distance.

This was when he felt closest to the passionate woman who intrigued him despite his best intentions.

Logic said she could be trouble. But Damen had been careful and sensible for a long, long time. Would it be so wrong to give free rein to this attraction?

Damen shook his head. 'Charming as your casual clothes are, they won't do. You're my girlfriend now.'

Though if she really were he'd be happy for her to dress as she did.

His gaze dropped to the cropped red and white top that barely reached her waist. She looked feisty, fresh and sexy. He'd found it almost impossible to keep his hand firm on the waistband of her jeans and not let it slide under the loose-fitting top to her warm flesh. Not because he didn't want to but because he didn't want to spook her. She was already jittery.

As far as he personally was concerned, Stephanie didn't need couture clothes. She was alluring whatever she wore. But this was about image.

Predictably her hands jammed onto her hips and her chin tilted. 'Because your high-class friends wouldn't believe we're an item? Are you ashamed to be seen with me as I am?'

'I'm not ashamed, Stephanie.' It was something quite different he felt when he was with her.

Would she feel so confident surrounded by socialites wearing expensive fashions? This wasn't just about looking good for the press but protecting Stephanie from condescension. Not from his friends or family. They wouldn't care, but there'd be others who'd underrate her because of her simple clothing choices. Damen refused to put her in that position.

He sighed. Why must she make this tough? Pride he understood but surely she was eager to get spending.

'Do you have an outfit for a wedding?'

Her brow crinkled. He could almost see her reviewing the contents of the single suitcase she'd brought.

'Your bridesmaid's dress is very attractive—' that was a masterly understatement, given the effect the sight of her in it had on his libido '—but as my girlfriend you'd have something new for the wedding we're attending at the end of next week.'

'You didn't mention a wedding.'

'I'm mentioning it now. And there'll be social events in Athens. The women will wear designer originals, high heels, jewellery, that sort of thing.' He paused. 'Have you got something suitable in your luggage?'

'Of course not. I came for a relaxed holiday on Corfu.'

'Then you'll feel more comfortable with a new wardrobe.'

Her gaze drifted from his and colour rose in her cheeks. 'I can't afford designer clothes.'

Damen stared. He'd just deposited a million dollars in her account. Surely she could afford a couple of dresses?

The silence lengthened and his patience wore thin. Stephanie was playing this part for the money, he understood that, but was she intent on screwing every cent she could from him?

Memories stirred of another woman who'd milked him for cash. And he, young and besotted, hadn't seen her for what she was till it was almost too late.

Damen's jaw gritted, his nostrils flaring in disdain as the woman before him stood silent, her eyes not quite meeting his.

So much for believing her to be difficult but fundamentally honest. It seemed she too was grasping when it came to getting her hands on his money.

He bent in a mocking bow, hiding his disappointment

with a grim smile. 'Then allow me, *kopela mou*. I'll buy the clothes you need. But I reserve a buyer's right to choose.' His smile widened. 'It will be a pleasure, dressing you.'

CHAPTER FIVE

STEPHANIE MET THAT glittering stare and wolfish smile and felt about an inch tall. Damen made her feel like a commodity he'd bought for his pleasure.

He talked about dressing her but the rapacious gleam in his eyes spoke of undressing.

She swallowed the knot of discomfort blocking her throat. He was aiming to unsettle her because she'd annoyed him. Fortunately she was wise to the fact his supposed attraction was a sham.

That didn't make her feel better.

It didn't take a genius to see Damen thought she angled to get whatever she could from this deal. He thought her a gold-digger.

She opened her mouth to explain then stopped. She had no intention of explaining the tangle of her financial affairs to this incredibly successful businessman. If she said she no longer had the money he'd pepper her with questions. The fiasco of her failed business venture, stolen funds and, above all, her grandmother's precarious financial position because she'd trusted Steph—no, she wasn't ready to share all that.

Pride rescued her.

'Thanks, Damen. I'm quite capable of choosing an outfit for a wedding. Though you have the right of veto, since this is your scheme and you know the people.' Anxiety shimmered through her at the thought of parading in unfamiliar finery amongst a crowd of sophisticates, pretending to be someone she wasn't. Steph wasn't and never would be a glamazon. She knew what she looked good in but her knowledge of designer originals was zero. 'Other than that, I'll get by with what I've brought.'

It wouldn't be pleasant. She knew cheap and cheerful

would only go so far when surrounded by elegant and rich, but she'd get by. She'd never see these people again and if they were so hung up on her wardrobe they weren't people she wanted to know.

Damen's eyes narrowed as if her words puzzled him. 'You'll arouse suspicion if you don't dress like my lover.'

Steph raised her eyebrows. 'You expect me to wear a negligee in public?' She had no doubt his women wore silk and lace, enticing and scanty.

Instead of responding in anger, Damen smiled, a slow, heart-kicking smile that made her legs wobble.

How did he do that when she was annoyed with him?

'I prefer my women to be discreet in public. It's a different matter in private, of course.'

Steph searched for a crushing response but he spoke first.

'How about a compromise? Wear your clothes when you're alone but when you're out with me wear something new, which I'll buy. Yes?'

She wanted to say no. Agreeing would cement his belief that she grasped for every penny she could get. But reason prevailed. She'd look out of place if she stuck to her guns. That would only make her more uncomfortable.

Reluctantly she nodded. 'Okay. A couple of outfits.'

The shopping expedition didn't start well.

Steph's heart sank as the limousine stopped in a street that screamed wealth and exclusivity. Damen gestured to a boutique with a single dress in the window, a dress that even Steph with her limited knowledge knew was a couture original. She swallowed. It was so unlike the chain stores she frequented. Appallingly she felt nervous.

Worse, she felt like a complete fraud.

She *was* a fraud. She was embarking on a big, fat lie.

She just hoped no one would get hurt as a result. Despite Damen's assurances she wondered if his female friend truly had no hopes of a permanent relationship. How would she feel when she saw Steph with Damen?

Steph stepped onto the heat of the Athens pavement, telling herself not to be intimidated. Yet a lifetime of scrimping, determined to avoid the financial difficulties that had beset her mother, had its downside. Steph was used to searching for bargains, not dropping a wad of money on the latest fashions.

'Sorry, Stephanie. I have to take this call.' Damen looked at his phone. 'You start and I'll join you.'

Steph lifted her chin, intensely aware that her dusky pink cotton sundress and flat sandals were out of place here. Memories hovered, of early years when she'd been teased by schoolmates about her ill-fitting clothes, cast-offs her mother had found at a charity shop.

But only for a moment. It had been a long time since she let anyone make her feel uncomfortable because of what she could or couldn't afford.

Yet her heart sank as she entered the shop with its plush, pale carpet and hushed atmosphere. Even the air smelled different. Expensive. Two saleswomen turned, poised, elegant and wearing polite smiles that dimmed as they took her in.

Her *'Kalimera'* was greeted with a cool nod from the older woman and a stare from the younger. Stephanie made herself walk further into the store, towards a sparsely populated rack of clothes. She hadn't reached it when the older saleswoman stepped forward, planting herself before the clothes.

'Can I help you with something specific?' She spoke English, clearly pegging her as a foreigner.

Steph told herself she imagined the protective way the woman stood between her and the rack.

'Thanks. I want a dress, but I prefer to browse.'

After a moment the woman moved aside, hovering too close as Steph examined the clothes.

That was just the beginning. Every time she moved,

one of the women shadowed her. When she paused near a display of handbags, all ostentatiously embellished with a well-known couturier's logo, the younger saleswoman deliberately blocked her path.

Steph's eyes widened. She'd told herself she was oversensitive but she didn't imagine this. They thought her a potential shoplifter. Heat filled her cheeks and she was torn between outrage and embarrassment. Outrage won.

She opened her mouth to speak when a deep voice made her turn.

'Stephanie? Is everything okay?'

Damen stood in the doorway, wide shoulders silhouetted against the sunshine. But there was enough light from the overhead chandelier to see he wasn't happy. That chiselled jaw was tight and a scowl marred his handsome face.

'What's going on here?' His tone was peremptory, but his ire wasn't directed at her. Steph watched the saleswomen stiffen and their eyes widen as he surveyed them. It was a look that could freeze at fifty paces.

'Nothing's going on,' Steph said, her voice a little overloud. There was no way she'd buy clothing here. Her skin crawled at how they'd made her feel. 'I can't see anything I want to wear.'

Damen stalked across the room, his gaze now focused on her, and she felt a glow begin deep inside. Long fingers threaded through hers as he stood close and heat spread through her whole body.

'You're sure? If there's something you want…' He waved towards the handbags.

Instantly the younger saleswoman stepped aside, her smile wide but lacking the smug confidence she'd shown before. 'This is a very exclusive range.' Her words tripped over themselves with eagerness. 'We're the only stockists in the country and I'm sure madam—'

Steph interrupted. She couldn't stand that fake friendliness. 'No, thanks. They're not my style.'

Damen looked from her to the other women and then to the leather goods. 'You're right. They're too gaudy. You don't need to wear someone else's name on your accessories to look good, *agapi mou*. Leave them for someone who feels the need to buy attention.'

Steph swallowed a gasp that was part giggle as she saw the other woman's eyes bulge. But it was true. The bags might be the latest must-have fashion but they were little more than advertisements for the designer whose logo was emblazoned on them so prominently.

Damen whisked her outside, not lowering his voice as he promised to take her somewhere with a better selection.

'You don't need to hold me so tight,' she murmured as they marched down the street.

'Sorry.' His grip on her arm eased and he slowed. 'That pair—'

'Forget them. They're not worth worrying about. I was about to leave when you arrived. There really was nothing there I wanted.' She refused to be treated that way.

Nevertheless, she admitted to herself at least, seeing Damen angry on her behalf made her feel good. She didn't need him to rescue her. She could fend for herself. But his protectiveness, for that was what it had been, warmed her.

Especially since Steph had seen their horror at Damen's scathing words and dismissive look. It was clear they'd recognised him or at least his air of authority, a man who expected and got the best.

Which set that nervous feeling going again in her stomach. She still had the ordeal of another high-end boutique to face.

But contrary to expectations she fared better in the next shop. It was just as exclusive with its white-on-white minimalism, stylish décor and vast arrangements of lilies scenting the air. But Steph was welcomed by a woman with a sincere smile. Even better, as well as clothes in the pale shades that had featured in the last place, the hangers also held bright colours.

Steph gravitated towards them, her hand lifting towards a fall of shimmering turquoise silk.

'How about this?' Damen picked up a dress in chic shades of cream and camel.

Steph's 'No, thanks,' coincided with the saleswoman declaring it was the wrong colour palette for her.

Damen suppressed a smile of satisfaction as Stephanie's expression lightened when the boutique owner insisted she should wear bold colours. Soon the pair were nodding, murmuring about cut and colour as they pored over the floor stock.

Clearly she'd got over her apparent unwillingness to get a new wardrobe. He'd thought she would.

Yet Damen was curious about their disagreement on the yacht. He'd sensed her protest about new clothes wasn't just so she didn't look too eager. As if he really had dented her pride.

He settled in a chair and drew out his phone, skimming messages. But he read none, his attention all on Stephanie.

He'd seen her frozen look of dismay in the last boutique and something inside him had given way. He'd wanted to savage the woman who'd put that expression on her face. As much as he'd wanted to hold and comfort Stephanie.

Except her rigid expression reminded him of the way she'd been with him in Melbourne. After they'd kissed. Her look had made him feel like he'd betrayed her. Despite the bigger picture and his need to help his best friend find his missing wife.

Now he felt like he'd done it again. Hurt her.

Why? Because he'd paid her to play a role? He hadn't forced her hand. Or because he'd left her alone with those snobby witches down the street?

Stephanie could stand up for herself. She didn't need

him as a champion. Damen remembered Emma saying her friend was strong and independent, that Stephanie had stuck up for her when they'd been kids together.

Yet his conscience prickled. And something else. Something more than guilt.

Whether he was responsible or not, Damen didn't want to see her look like that again, pale with distress. Her barbs he could cope with. He almost enjoyed them. Her rare smiles ditto. But that frozen look of stunned hurt pierced something behind his ribs.

Fortunately movement from the rear of the boutique distracted him from his churning thoughts. The saleswoman stepped back from the changing room, looking satisfied. She was followed by...

Damen breathed deep and told himself to ignore the strange little jitter that made his pulse uneven.

It was simply Stephanie dressed up. Not in a pretty bridesmaid's gown. In an outfit designed with one aim. To seduce.

He'd seen his share of seductive women. Had bedded them too. Yet the sight of Stephanie in that clinging outfit sent a blow to the solar plexus that hampered his breathing.

It was a jumpsuit. Was that what you called it? That sounded too prim and old-fashioned for this. She wore silky material that wasn't red and wasn't dark pink but somewhere in between. The neckline lifted to a high collar, but her shoulders were completely bare and there was a narrow slit down between her breasts that gave teasing glimpses of her cleavage. A cleavage that seemed unfettered by a bra. The fabric clung to her waist and hips before falling in loose folds to her feet. Feet encased in high-heeled sandals. She looked fabulous. Sophisticated and effortlessly sexy.

Except he knew the high tilt of that chin. He'd learned that pugnacious angle could signal anger or doubt.

Damen got to his feet, his phone falling. 'You don't like it?'

She swung around, drawing a breath that made her breasts rise against the thin fabric. Heat stirred low in his body. He kept his eyes on hers and read what looked like concern.

She bit her lip and lifted those slender bare shoulders.

It was ridiculous. Except for her arms and shoulders she was covered to her toes. Yet the sight of that flesh, looking velvety soft against the contrasting material, seemed more enticing than if she'd worn a bikini.

'I'm not sure.' Her gaze turned to the full-length mirrors at the back of the room and Damen caught an expression that hovered between wistful and worried.

'It might have been made for you, madam,' the sales-woman said. 'That colour is perfect.'

Still Stephanie looked uncomfortable.

Damen cleared his throat. 'I like it.' Too much. Far, far too much. He looked at her in that slinky, flirty outfit and imagined what she'd look like without it. Without anything. 'You don't?'

In the mirror Stephanie's gaze snared his and his throat dried.

'It's not me, is it? I mean, it's beautiful.' She smoothed her hands down the fabric. 'But it's designed for someone more...'

Damen wasn't used to Stephanie tentative or uncertain. She was forthright to the point of driving him crazy.

'More what?' His voice hit a gravelly note as he took in her slightly lost look. 'It's a perfect fit.' Too perfect but he couldn't complain, for that would be admitting the sight of her in it tied his libido in knots. 'You look classy and sexy.'

'I do?' Her eyes widened.

The saleswoman, after a look at Damen, excused herself and headed back to the changing room.

Damen stared at the sultry figure in the mirror. Two hours ago he'd been annoyed with Stephanie and the way she seemed bent on screwing him for every cent she could. What had happened to his anger?

She hadn't asked for sympathy. If anything she'd down-played that scene in the other shop. Yet her nervous expression made him pause, and not just because she looked good enough to eat.

Was it possible Stephanie doubted herself in that outfit? Surely that was impossible. He strode across to stand behind her. 'What's the problem? Isn't it comfortable?'

She shook her head. 'It feels gorgeous to wear.' Was that longing in her tone?

Damen stepped in, so close the scent of warm vanilla teased his nostrils. 'Then we'll take it.'

'It's not too…?' She made a vague gesture.

'Too?' He was tempted to agree that she looked too disturbingly sexy. He didn't want other men to see her dressed like this. But Damen wasn't stupid enough to reveal that.

Fascinated, he saw a hint of colour at the base of her throat. Her gaze slid to a point in the mirror near his shoulder. When she spoke the words were clipped. 'I've never worn haute couture. You probably need a certain air to carry it off, to be glamorous and…' Her words petered out with a shrug. 'I'm afraid I look like someone playing dress-up, someone who doesn't belong in such clothes.'

Something tugged at Damen's chest. His eyes narrowed. Was she serious? Stephanie always seemed so confident.

He saw that flush rise higher. He doubted even the best actress could blush at will.

'What you look like, Stephanie, is an attractive, desirable woman. The clothes look great on you but that's window dressing. You looked fabulous in cut-off jeans and bare feet.' He paused as she swung to face him. Her velvety eyes rounded.

For a long moment she didn't say anything. Then a smile curled the corners of her mouth and her shadowed expression morphed into one of pleasure. For Damen, standing so close, the impact of her smile was palpable.

'You made me think my appearance didn't meet your exacting standards, Mr Nicolaides.'

Damen shook his head, entranced by the way she smiled with her whole face. He wondered what it would be like to have her look at him that way regularly. Damen liked it. Too much.

'I never said that. I just want you dressed appropriately for the occasion.'

She tilted her head as if trying to read more than his words. Then she nodded once, her manner turning businesslike, that warm glow quenched as if it had never been. 'Okay. How many outfits do I need?'

Steph was incredibly glad Damen had insisted on new clothes, though she hated the idea of him buying them.

There was something suggestive about a man paying for what she wore. As if he'd bought her too. The idea had made her feel grubby at first, until she saw he was right—she was more comfortable mixing with these well-dressed people wearing what she thought of as her camouflage.

At least she didn't look like a charity case.

Steph washed her hands and told herself he paid her to play a part but he hadn't bought *her*. Even if it felt like it on occasions like this, at his friend's party in a spectacular house looking over Athens and the coast.

Damen was as good as his promise, never kissing her, but whenever they were together in public each look, each touch, even the slightly deeper tone he adopted when speaking to her, gave the impression they were lovers.

He was so adept at it sometimes she found it hard to remember it was an act.

The first night, at the cocktail party opening of a new museum wing, Steph had been fazed by his faux intimacy, struggling to play her part and respond in kind.

What worried her now, after more than a week, was how easily she'd grown accustomed to it.

Looking away from her accusing eyes in the mirror of the guest bathroom, Steph busied herself reviving her lipstick.

She should be able to take this charade in her stride now. Damen stuck to their agreement and she was gradually getting used to the bustle of Athens as she explored the sights each day, chauffeured by his driver.

Instead her uneasiness grew. Oh, she was having a ball exploring this amazing city. That was an experience she'd carry for the rest of her days. But the more time she spent with Damen the more he undercut her prejudice against him. Yesterday he'd even come home early to drive her to Cape Sounion to watch the sunset. She knew he'd done it so they could be seen together, yet Steph hugged to herself a secret delight that he'd been prompted by her saying she wanted to see the famous temple ruins.

They spent every evening together and he was not only attentive but also considerate, charming and with a vein of dry humour that appealed too much. Just the sort of man she could imagine being attracted to.

He was too good an actor, she told herself, remembering how he'd feigned interest in her before. When he'd tried to milk her for information.

She put the lipstick away and surveyed herself. She wore the boldly coloured outfit she'd tried on that first day. Its fragile silk clung to her breasts and hips and swished around her legs like a caress.

Crazy how for a couple of minutes in the boutique she'd been racked by self-doubt. As if she were still the scrawny kid in second-hand clothes who never fitted in. She'd thought she'd got over that self-consciousness, the fear of being judged and found wanting. Steph had buried that sense of being second-best with years of hard work and achievement. She believed in her ability to build the future she wanted, to be the woman she wanted to be.

Yet as she'd stood there, wearing this stunning outfit only the rich could afford, she'd felt out of her depth. Suddenly it wasn't just her ability to play this masquerade that she doubted, but herself. Jared's betrayal, her gullibility in being sucked in by a fraud, losing everything she'd worked for, had smashed her confidence. She'd got the wobbles.

Till Damen's words and the look in his eyes reassured her. She remembered the swelling warmth unfurling through her at his male appreciation. He'd told her she was desirable and she'd seen proof in his body language and gleaming eyes.

Steph didn't need a man's opinion to feel good about herself. Nor did she care for people who'd judge her on how she looked.

Yet she was honest enough to admit that when Damen looked at her with that flare of heat, when she *felt* as much as saw his smile as he took in her appearance, it did wonderful things for her bruised ego.

That had to be why she didn't mind those admiring looks from him. Not because she wanted Damen to want her. That would be disastrous. But because it was balm to her wounded soul.

Steph squared her shoulders and opened the door. Music reached her ears, and the hum of voices. She walked down the corridor and into the vast sitting room that could have swallowed her flat several times over.

Knots of people stood chatting and laughing, all elegant, all beautifully dressed. A few, glimpsed through open doors to the next room, danced. Jewels sparkled and the air was rich with expensive scents. But she couldn't see Damen's dark head above the rest.

Her host, a pleasantly ordinary man for a billionaire, caught her eye. 'You're looking for Damen? He's on the terrace.' He smiled. 'Unless you'd care to dance?'

'Thank you but no.' Steph softened her rejection with a smile.

The idea of dancing in these teetering heels terrified her. She loved the way they looked, making her legs seem so much longer, but dancing in them? She'd probably break her ankle and that would be the end of her attempts to be poised and glamorous.

She threaded through the crowd to the huge space where floor-to-ceiling windows were folded back, opening the room to the terrace and gardens.

There were fewer people here but Damen was easy to locate. Steph told herself it was because of his height but she had the disquieting feeling it was more. Even at a crowded event, on the rare occasions they got separated, she always knew precisely where he was. She had the feeling it worked both ways. More than once she'd seen him look up from a conversation, his gaze unerringly catching hers. Steph wasn't sure whether to be flattered or worried by that.

This time, though, he didn't notice her. He stood at the far edge of the paved terrace, away from other guests, and his attention was on someone beside him, his head inclined as they spoke.

Steph started forward then paused, taking in the scene. There was something about their body language, how close they stood. They didn't touch yet it was obvious even from a distance that they shared an intimacy.

Even in the gloom, with her face averted, it was clear Damen's companion was incredibly beautiful.

She was everything Steph wasn't. Tall and effortlessly poised, as if she was used to holding her own at sophisticated parties full of celebrities and the ultra-wealthy. Her hair was blonde and straight, worn in one of those apparently casual styles that combined an elegant knot with sexy wisps around her neck. She wore a strapless gown that revealed endless legs. She was stunning.

Gazing at her, Steph was aware of the unfamiliarity of her high heels. Of the unruly mass of curls clustered around her head. She'd planned to get a haircut in Athens, thinking even a gamine cut was preferable to her natural look, but Damen had forestalled her, saying she looked charming.

Sophisticated and gorgeous beat charming hands down.

Steph hated the little corkscrew of hurt as memories surfaced, of being ridiculed about her appearance, because poverty *looked* different. But that was then and this was now. Steph hadn't been that girl for a long, long time.

Besides, this wasn't a competition.

Damen was merely talking to the woman.

Yet their ease together, the way their heads angled as if they were sharing secrets, made Steph wonder if *this* was the woman he went to so much trouble for. The woman he insisted wasn't his lover.

Steph began walking, swallowing a bitter taste in her mouth.

Damen's head turned, eyes fixing on her.

She felt that stare like the scrape of a blade over her bare arms and shoulders, like a hand sliding, slow and deliberate, over the flimsy silk that covered her body. He made her feel supremely aware of her body in a way no other man had. It was scary and exciting at the same time.

And it infuriated her that, even now, when she'd interrupted him with another woman, Steph was ultra-aware of him. Not out of self-defence, but with that trembling feminine awareness he'd stirred in her from the first. The awareness that had allowed him to make a fool of her.

Steph was mortified at how he could unsettle her. Her skin flushed and her insides rippled with nerves. She was like a silly sixteen-year-old facing the object of her first crush.

When she stopped it wasn't Damen who broke the silence, but the woman who stepped forward with a welcoming smile.

'Steph, it's great to see you again!'

Steph inhaled a scent of cinnamon and roses, felt the

brush of soft skin and softer hair as the woman kissed her on the cheek.

Steph blinked. 'Clio?'

They'd met the previous week on Corfu. The Greek woman was a friend of Emma and Christo's and Steph had liked her.

Her heart dropped like a stone through water.

She'd told herself it didn't matter who the woman was that Damen cared about so much that he'd go to ridiculous lengths to protect her.

But it did matter.

Clio wasn't just gorgeous and sophisticated. From the little Steph had seen and heard, she knew Clio was kind-hearted, clever and nice. The sort of woman a man was drawn to not just for a fling but for life.

Even if Damen didn't want to marry yet, Clio was the sort of woman who'd fit into his world and make him happy.

She was perfect for him.

What Steph didn't understand was the pang of hurt that lanced from her chest to her stomach. A ripping pain that skewered her to the spot and caught her breath.

Almost as if she was envious.

CHAPTER SIX

STEPHANIE WAS QUIET on the drive home. Not relaxed, but humming with tension. Damen could read her more easily now, even when she tried to keep her feelings to herself. She was full of pent-up emotion. Had been ever since she'd seen Clio.

Silently he sighed. Things had been going so well before that.

Stephanie hadn't been brittle in his company any more. She relaxed with him, smiled, and it was easier for them to play the part of lovers. Except for the frustration that rode him as he looked at her pretty mouth, remembered its taste, and his promise not to kiss her.

Until she invited him.

That day couldn't come soon enough.

Looking at her tight features as they entered his penthouse, he saw it was clear today wasn't that day.

The front door hadn't even closed before Steph swung round, her breasts swaying, bright silk flaring around her legs.

'Is she the one? Clio?' Her words were bullet fast.

Damen shut the door and led the way into the sitting room.

'Would you like a drink?' He poured himself an ouzo, for once not bothering with water. He wanted the burn of aniseed fire, hoping it might sear away his annoyance at her probing and the feeling of being on the brink of doing something irreversible. Damen had spent the evening drinking sparkling water because it was increasingly difficult to hold Stephanie close, pretend they were lovers, and not plant his mouth on hers.

'What I'd like is an answer.'

She stood, arms akimbo, head and shoulders thrust back, breasts forward. In the lamplight the silk was like flame licking her body, turning her into a fierce, sexy Amazon.

Damen tipped back his head and swallowed the ouzo in one mouthful. Fire ripped from his mouth down his throat to his belly. But it didn't quench the need vibrating through him. He slammed the glass down and stepped away.

Why had he thought alcohol would help? Nothing would help, except Stephanie in his arms, in his bed.

'What was the question?'

Her eyebrows rose. 'Is Clio the lover you're protecting with this masquerade? Or are you deceiving her?'

'You don't need to know who it is. That's irrelevant. Two million dollars' worth of irrelevant.' Why must she pester him about this?

Dark curls danced as Stephanie shook her head, her mouth drawing into a straight line. 'I won't be party to a scheme that's going to hurt anyone. I *like* Clio.'

'I've told you, no one will be harmed.' Impatience rose. Hadn't he assured her of that, explained why this charade was necessary? 'Believe me.'

Again she shook her head, her expression implacable.

'I can't.' This time she spoke softly, not gently but as if her voice stretched thin. 'Don't you understand? How can I trust you? You're a liar.'

The accusation was a punch to Damen's gut. He stood straighter, words of outrage forming. No one accused a Nicolaides of dishonour.

'Don't give me that intimidating stare! You know it's true. You don't get to be a multi-billionaire by playing nice. Who knows what sort of shady deals you do to make money?'

Damen stared, taken aback. Where had that come from? Simply because he was successful? Did she have something against businessmen?

'You made me leave Melbourne with you because of a lie that you knew where Emma was—'

'Only to get the truth from you.'

'And the next time I see you you offer me money to lie to your friends and family, to all the world for that matter.' Stephanie drew another, audible breath. 'How can I believe you? I need to *know* what's going on. All week I've wondered about every woman we meet. Is this the one? Or that one? Is she hurting seeing us together? I don't want to be party to a scheme to dupe someone. I should never have agreed to it.'

The wrathful words died on Damen's tongue. There was true distress in Stephanie's face and restlessly plaiting hands.

Everything inside him stilled as suspicion stirred.

'Because someone duped you? Hurt you?'

Stephanie's chin shot higher. Her hands clenched and her hunching shoulders pushed back again so she stood tall.

Yet it was there in her eyes. Acknowledgement. Though he guessed she'd die if she thought he could see it.

Damen's next breath was uneven, as if his lungs refused to work. The thought of someone betraying Stephanie, creating that wounded look, made him want to commit an act of violence.

But with that came the sober realisation that she spoke the truth. She had a right to know more. Especially as they were about to head into the lion's den, visiting Clio's family.

Damen was appalled that Stephanie believed him to be dishonest. It went against everything he stood for.

This had to be sorted.

Plus he wanted to find out about the person who'd harmed her.

Damen drew a slow breath. 'Take a seat, Stephanie.'

Steph sank onto a sofa. Her emotions were jumbled. She didn't understand why seeing Clio with Damen had disrupted her fragile equilibrium. Yet the suspicion they'd been, or perhaps still were, together changed everything.

'*Is* it Clio?'

He took a seat opposite, his arms on his thighs as he leaned forward. For a long time he regarded her enigmatically. Then, reluctantly, it seemed, he nodded.

Steph's heart sank.

'Don't look at me like that,' Damen growled. 'It's not what you think.'

He ploughed his fingers through glossy hair that fell perfectly back into place. Of course it did. Everything in this man's world worked the way he wanted. Business, money... Even women he barely knew agreed to put aside their principles to lie for him.

'Clio isn't and never has been my lover. She's like a sister. In fact, since she's nearer to my age, in some ways she's closer to me than they are.'

'You have sisters?' Steph could have done an internet search on his family but she'd felt that the less she knew about him the better. So far ignorance hadn't provided any protection. She was involved, more involved than was safe.

'Two sisters, one studying in the States and one working overseas.' He paused. 'But my mother's in Greece. You'll meet her at the wedding.'

'Not your father?'

Damen's eyebrows arrowed down. 'He died. A long time ago.'

Maybe that accounted for Damen's innate air of authority, as if he was long used to people jumping to do his bidding.

'I'm sorry.' It was an automatic response, yet that frown told her his father's death still evoked emotions.

'Clio and I are related. Her father is my mother's cousin. Manos is a decent man. He was even something of a mentor when I took over from my father.' Steph noted a twitch of the eyebrows as if the memory of that time wasn't easy.

'Perhaps that gave him expectations where there should be none, because of the bond between our families. He's also extremely obstinate. Once he gets an idea he's likely to steamroller people into agreeing with him.'

Not unlike Damen. But Steph kept the observation to herself.

'Now he believes Clio and I should marry. He's a traditionalist and Clio is his eldest, yet it's her younger sister, Cassie, marrying this weekend and that doesn't sit well. He wants Clio to marry and settle down soon. Plus,' Damen spread his hands, 'he'd like to see the Nicolaides money benefit his family. He thinks I've reached an age where I'm looking for a bride.'

Something shifted in Steph's middle. It wasn't a pain but there was definite discomfort. It had to be due to tension. It had nothing to do with the idea of Damen searching for a wife. That was none of her business.

'That doesn't explain why he thinks you and Clio might marry.'

Damen rolled his shoulders as if they were tight. 'Clio and I have an informal arrangement.'

Steph's stomach lurched as she imagined that agreement. Her own experience was limited but she could imagine Damen enjoying a casual sexual relationship with the lovely Clio. She sat further back on the seat, away from the man watching her so intently.

'Not what you're thinking.'

'You have no idea what I'm thinking!'

He shook his head. 'When you're annoyed or offended you purse your mouth and your nose scrunches up. Despite what I've already told you, despite the fact Clio wasn't in the least jealous, seeing you with me tonight, you've decided we're having an affair. We're not.'

His laser-sharp stare dared her to disagree. Steph said nothing, too concerned about his ability to read her so easily.

'Clio is establishing her interior-design business, and

going out with me is a way to network with wealthy potential clients. Plus we like each other's company. I can relax
and laugh with her.'

He couldn't relax with other women? It sounded odd, but
perhaps wealthy men found it hard to make true friends.
Maybe that was why Damen and Christo were close. Each
knew the other wasn't angling to benefit financially from
their friendship. It struck Steph that living with a fortune
had downsides she'd never considered.

'Clio knows I'm just a pretend girlfriend?'

'I didn't tell her and she didn't ask. A party isn't the
place for confidences, especially as the aim is to make the
world believe you and I are an item. But, as she begged for
help last week to get her father off her back, she probably
guessed. You're my way of helping her.' He paused. 'I can
give you her number if you want, though I suspect she'd
prefer not to talk about her family troubles with someone
she barely knows.'

Steph blinked, digesting that. It should sound ridiculous.
Instead she found it...plausible.

'I see.' He didn't care if she contacted Clio and it was
true Clio hadn't seemed disturbed to see them together. It
must be a strong friendship for him to go to such lengths.
'But you have no qualms, lying to everyone else, including your mother?'

Damen folded his arms and surveyed her down that imperious nose like a judge examining a prisoner. Once more
she felt she was pushing her luck, pursuing this. But she had
to know. Despite how easy it was to feign intimacy with
Damen, she hated being party to deception.

'I won't lie to my mother. Nor do I want her thinking I'll
marry when I have no intention of ever taking a wife. I'll
tell her what she needs to know.'

Steph was torn between wondering why Damen was
anti-marriage and a prickling of hurt pride at the idea of
his family viewing her as expendable. They'd believe he'd

picked her up for a short fling. That she wasn't good enough to be considered for anything else.

But she'd been well paid to play that part. She couldn't afford to be offended or embarrassed.

'Satisfied?' His sensuous mouth curled up at one side.

Steph despised the way she noticed such things, responding to his allure. If she didn't, this would be much easier.

Reluctantly she nodded. She still had questions but she believed what he'd said. Why lie? Especially when she could get the truth from Clio.

'Good. Now tell me why you're so ready to believe the worst of me. I admit we got off to a rocky start in Melbourne. But it's more than that. You don't trust easily.'

Steph met that unblinking stare and wondered how many of her secrets this man had read. Most people saw her as bright and friendly and didn't realise how hard she found it to put her trust in others, especially men.

He turned the tables on her, putting her on the defensive.

'Was it a man?'

She couldn't prevent her flinch. Jared's deception was too recent, too raw. But she hid it, she hoped, with a shrug, horrified at how Damen had pinpointed her weak spot so easily. 'Just because I question your motives doesn't mean I have difficulty trusting people.'

He lifted his eyebrows.

'Besides, my past is my own business. It doesn't concern you.'

'So it was a man. What did he do? Leave you for another woman? Or was he married and you didn't know?'

Steph stifled her automatic response, that it was typical of a man to assume the betrayal was sexual. What would Damen say if he realised she'd never been with a man? She learned to be wary of trusting too much. Besides, instead of going out dating she'd spent almost every waking hour working so she could be totally independent.

'You've got it wrong.'

'Have I?' Again Damen leaned towards her and she had the crazy idea those narrowed eyes saw everything she kept hidden.

'Let's just say I've had my fill of unscrupulous people, ready to do anything to get ahead.'

Her words hit home, for Damen's expression turned dark.

Maybe she should apologise, explain that for once she didn't mean him. But that would lead to demands for explanations and she was exhausted. Steph didn't have the stamina for more.

Tonight had been an emotional minefield. She believed Damen's explanation about Clio but that didn't make their situation easier. It seemed more perilous with every hour they were together.

Steph shot to her feet, wobbling a little on her heels. 'I'm tired. I'll see you in the morning.'

Damen stood too. One long stride closed the gap between them.

There it was again, that shiver of awareness racking her body. To her horror Steph felt her nipples bud against gossamer-fine silk.

Did he notice? His eyes held hers but she saw heat flicker in his expression. His gaze dropped to her mouth and it felt like a caress, there on her lips. All night he'd looked at her mouth in a way that made her tremble with expectation. Made her want him to kiss her.

Did he move closer or did she sway towards him?

Abruptly she stepped away, turning for the door, heart pounding in her throat. 'Goodnight, Damen.'

Would he follow? Reach for her? Forget the contract he'd signed and kiss her?

She wanted him to. Wanted it with a self-destructive force that scared her. Her breath snagged as she waited, pulse thundering, for his touch.

But he made no move. She was almost at the corridor to the bedrooms when he spoke.

'Don't forget we leave early tomorrow.'

'I won't forget.'

How could she? She'd barely got through ten days pretending to be his lover and she was about to head to an island wedding where she'd have to play the part to perfection.

The worrying thing was that part of her wished it were true. That they were lovers. She was tying herself in knots trying to quell this attraction.

Steph no longer hated Damen, could no longer rely on negativity to keep her safe. Tonight he'd taken her into his confidence, naming names and explaining facts about his personal life that she sensed he hated revealing.

Yet he'd done it because he accepted she needed to know. He'd heard her qualms and put her needs above his own desire for privacy. That meant a lot. It also changed the dynamic between them.

This attraction she'd tried to conquer was burrowing deeper than doubt or conscience. Alarmingly, it grew stronger rather than weaker the more she discovered about him.

'You're kidding, right? The whole idea of bringing your mega-yacht was so you could stay on it, surely?' They reached the end of the path and Stephanie swung to face him, her eyes sparking.

Damen knew he should be focused on other things, like handling Manos, who, while ostensibly welcoming, was suspicious and far from happy. Or his own mother, who, despite being told the truth about Stephanie, had regarded the pair of them through today's pre-wedding party with a speculative twinkle that spelled trouble. Or even solving the puzzle of who'd hurt Stephanie so badly, creating that deep-running vein of distrust that she used to keep him at a distance.

But he couldn't concentrate on those things. The late-afternoon breeze teased Stephanie's summery dress and played with those dark curls in a way that made him wish he were free to touch her. Not for the benefit of an audience, but for mutual pleasure.

His belly tightened as he imagined her lifting her pouting lips to his.

Her skin was sun-kissed and, he knew, silky soft. The dress, a floaty thing in white, decorated with cornflowers, accentuated her tiny waist and delectable figure. The cornflower-blue sandal straps tied around her delicate ankles kept drawing his attention to her legs.

'Damen? Are you listening?'

'I am.' And looking. And smelling too. For, as well as the salt scent borne off the water a few hundred metres away, he inhaled Stephanie's warm, vanilla perfume. It was wholesome yet sexy and had a direct line to his libido.

Damen shoved his hands in his pockets and looked at the guest house behind her. Set away from the mansion that was Clio's family home, it perched on a low cliff above the beach.

'I'm sure it's comfortable. Clio refurbished it.'

'It's not the comfort I'm worried about. It's the size. It looks small.'

It was. Bright white like most traditional houses in the Cyclades Islands and surely no bigger than a few rooms. The door gleamed blue, matching the pair of chairs on a tiny terrace positioned to take in the view. Pink geraniums frothed from matching blue pots.

It was charming.

And small, very small.

Damen looked away to his yacht moored in the bay. That was where they should be spending the next two nights. In separate staterooms. Instead...

Damen suppressed a frisson of anticipation.

'It's generous of Manos to offer us the guest house during the wedding celebrations. I couldn't refuse.'

'Of course you could refuse. You're Damen Nicolaides! You run a shipping empire. You make billion-dollar decisions.'

He bit back a laugh. 'Thanks for the pep talk. But this isn't business, this is family, and consequently far more complicated and important.'

He thought of Manos's almost bullish attitude as he'd hosted today's pre-wedding lunch for extended family. Of Clio's set jaw and brittle air and her mother's drawn face. Only Cassie, the bride-to-be, had looked happy.

To refuse Manos's hospitality on such an occasion would have been to insult him. Manos had given him helpful guidance in the turbulent time when Damen had unexpectedly inherited Nicolaides Shipping. His family had supported Damen's in that time of terrible grief. Manos's company and personal wealth hadn't fared as well in the last decade as Damen's, not that he'd reveal that on the occasion of his daughter's wedding. But to have Damen, younger, far wealthier and more successful, the relative he'd once helped in a time of crisis, reject his personal invitation...

Damen refused to do it. Besides, a suspicion had grown today that Clio had arranged the invitation to ram home to her stubborn father that Stephanie was Damen's lover, not a casual friend. One thing was certain—this secluded guest house was designed for intimacy.

Stephanie tilted her head as if seeing him for the first time.

'I'd rather stay on the *Amphitrite* too, but I can't insult Manos by refusing his hospitality.'

If it *had* been Manos's idea originally, he'd probably hoped having Damen stay on the premises would be a chance to pressure him into an engagement with Clio.

'Because it would hurt his pride?'

'Something like that.' Damen wondered how he'd let things get so far. How he hadn't realised his relatives had unrealistic expectations of a match.

'Come on.' He opened the door. 'Let's see what it's like.'

It was worse than he'd thought.

Or, depending on your perspective, he realised, better.

Clio had made the place a sumptuous escape. Wide floor-boards gleamed beneath their feet, extending to a wall of windows. From here you could see only sky and the sea, from aquamarine shallows through shades of turquoise to sapphire depths. A soaring ceiling and simple but luxurious furnishings added to the sense of space. As did the lack of internal walls.

The living space swept around the curve of the cliff. Set in a semi-circular alcove to the left, in front of more windows, was a large bath designed for two, a platform beside it holding towels and an ice bucket. On the other side, in a large alcove with its own set of panoramic windows, was a wide bed, dressed in shades of cream, turquoise and blue.

Damen heard Stephanie's breath hitch. She marched past, surveying first the open bathing area then the bedroom that wasn't a room. The stupendous view she ignored. She opened a door, but it revealed only a fridge and a benchtop with a state-of-the-art coffee machine. Another door opened into a walk-in wardrobe. A third led to a bathroom containing only a toilet and a pair of washbasins.

'Two sinks but they can't afford a wall around the bath!'

Damen's lips twitched. 'The open feel is very popular. I'm told it maximises space.'

'And minimises privacy.' Stephanie strode past him, investigating the sofa and chairs placed to make the most of the view. 'There's not even a pull-out mattress.'

Damen's smile vanished as he registered her distress. 'It will be fine. It's just two nights.'

She spun to face him, hands on hips.

'This isn't a joke. If you think for one minute I'm going to share a bed with you—'

'Of course not.' Damen raised his hands. He was too sensible to admit that his first thought on seeing that massive bed and luxurious bath was to imagine sharing both with Stephanie. Stephanie in his arms, warm, willing and eager for his loving.

He repressed a shiver of arousal that arrowed straight to his groin, and kept his expression bland.

'This isn't a trick to compromise you.'

For a taut second she held his stare, then nodded once and turned away. Damen was surprised at the pleasure he felt knowing she believed him. It was a start, a small one, but important. He'd been stunned in Athens to discover how deep her distrust ran.

And the fact that he wanted her in his bed?

He had every intention of achieving that but not by trickery.

'I could sleep on the sofa,' she said.

Over his dead body. What sort of man did she think him? Actually, it was probably best not to go there.

'You have the bed and I'll take the sofa.' Earnest brown eyes met his. 'Don't even think of arguing, Stephanie.' His pride wouldn't let him sleep in comfort while she bunked down there.

Finally she nodded and turned to the bed. 'They've brought our bags from the yacht. I suppose we should freshen up before this restaurant dinner.'

Damen saw her wistful glance at the massive bath.

She'd done marvellously all day, fielding questions from his extended family, playing his devoted girlfriend and doing it well. Stephanie had been attentive and friendly but not gushing. She'd coped with meeting not only his mother and Clio's family but also dozens of distant relatives, all excited and curious to meet his companion, for Damen was notorious for never bringing a woman to any family celebration.

But, while he'd grown more relaxed as the day wore on, Stephanie had become more tense. Her shoulders were set high and her breathing was shallow, as if she was on high alert.

'Why don't you relax and have a bath? We've got plenty of time and I have calls I need to make. I'll go down to the beach to make them and stretch my legs.'

'If you don't mind, that would be great.' Her smile was tentative but genuine and he felt as if he'd won a victory.

She turned and opened the case that his staff had packed and brought from the yacht.

A second later she was scrabbling to pick up the item on top, moving it from his view. But not before Damen saw a black, lacy bra that looked almost see-through in her hands. Next was a skimpy pair of matching knickers, which left him imagining Stephanie wearing sexy underwear and nothing else, posing for his approval as she had at that Athens boutique.

He sucked in his breath so sharply, pain jabbed his ribs. Heat drenched him.

Damen's ease disintegrated. And so did his amusement at her disapproval of this beautiful retreat.

It struck him that she wasn't the only one who'd be grateful for a barrier between them tonight. A convenient wall so he didn't have to watch her sleeping or lie awake calculating how many steps between the sofa and the bed.

Staying here together would be a special form of torture. Not because he couldn't cope with a sofa, but because, much as he wanted to seduce Stephanie, he refused to take advantage of a situation that made her nervous.

He had a long, frustrating night ahead.

CHAPTER SEVEN

THE MUSIC WOUND to a halt but Steph's heart kept pounding a matching rhythm. The traditional music had initially sounded slow, almost ponderous, but it had altered as the dance went on. Or maybe once she'd been tugged into the line of women holding hands, following the bride, she'd begun to notice extra nuances.

She'd been happy to sit at the outdoor table with its flickering candles and watch. She'd been fascinated by the beauty of what seemed simultaneously a simple dance yet at the same time intriguingly intricate. Women of all ages joined the growing line. There was one, iron-haired and sturdy-framed, who danced with the grace of a professional. There was the little girl in plaits, eyes round with excitement as she watched the bride.

Suddenly, without giving her time to think, there was Clio, pulling Steph from her seat, dragging her to join the throng. Steph had stumbled, protested, but the smiles and nods had drawn her in till she found the beat and then, heart swelling with delight, she hadn't wanted to stop. She'd felt not only welcome but also included, a real part of this joyous event.

She'd barely been aware of the men at the tables. This didn't feel like a dance performed to attract their attention, but something done for the participants, especially the bride. She met the smiling faces of the other women and grinned back. They'd all been so kind and friendly.

It had been the same all day. Except for a few women who'd looked at her when she arrived with Damen as if they'd like to claw her eyes out. But she'd received jealous glares like that in Athens. It came with the territory.

Damen's woman. That was how everyone saw her.

The knowledge set up a familiar thud in her chest. A thud that echoed the erratic pulse beat that had kept her from sleep last night.

She must have snatched some rest, for she'd woken scratchy-eyed to find Damen gone, for an early swim, she discovered later. But it felt as if she'd spent most of the night awake, listening to her drumming pulse, thinking how close he lay, how she wanted to go to him.

Would it have been the bravest thing she'd ever done or the stupidest?

All this flirting, the fleeting caresses and searing looks, was undermining her resistance. Logic said it was all for show. Something else, deep-buried and needy, declared those looks, that tension, the sparking heat when they touched, were more than playacting.

If only she had enough experience to know for sure.

The events of the last months had damaged her self-esteem but Steph wasn't by nature a shrinking violet.

She wanted Damen.

She'd given up trying to avoid that truth. The wanting drove her crazy. If the desire was mutual...

Her breath shuddered out. If it was *mutual* she'd be tempted to do what she'd never done and invite physical intimacy. Because surely that would be a way of getting rid of it. Like an itch that needed to be scratched. Because so far it was simply compounding, growing stronger and more distracting almost by the hour.

Except Steph recalled how easily Damen had feigned attraction. She refused to make that mistake twice. It was one of the reasons she'd been horrified to discover they had to share that sybaritically luxurious and far too small guest house.

She was caught, unable to be sure what he felt but unable to escape this increasingly urgent physical attraction.

She swung round to look for Damen. He was still where

she'd left him, but instead of watching her he was in conversation with a group of men.

Steph's heart sank. What had she expected? That he'd
be transfixed by the sight of her stumbling through a traditional Greek dance?

He'd spent the afternoon glued to her side. He'd been
the one to pick up her filmy shawl when it slid off on the
way to the church. She recalled the warmth of his hands as
he'd placed it around her shoulders and the whisper of his
breath tickling her face as he stood close and explained the
wedding ceremony. He'd spent the day playing the attentive lover, showing Manos and everyone else that he was
devoted to his new girlfriend. Was it any surprise his attention wandered now he was alone?

'May I?'

Steph swung around to meet melting dark eyes. The
guy's smile was wide and friendly and Steph felt none
of that jangling hyper-awareness that taunted her with
Damen.

What was more, he looked at her with an avid appreciation she knew was real. Today, when Damen had seen her in
her stunning new dress, ready for the wedding, he'd smiled
and said she looked perfect. But his gaze hadn't lingered
the way this guy's did. Damen had seemed distracted, as
if he had something else on his mind. Inevitably Steph decided she looked 'perfect' for her role as pretend girlfriend
but the sight left him unmoved.

'You'd like to dance? Yes? My name is Vassili. Come.'
He held out his hand, his smile widening. 'Let's have some
fun.'

Fun. How long since she'd had that? Always at the back
of her mind were worries.

Suppressing the need to check on Damen again—she
didn't need his approval—she smiled and put her hand in
Vassili's. 'My name is Steph.'

'I know. Stephanie. The most beautiful woman here.'

That smile became a beaming grin and suddenly Steph felt lighter than she had in ages. Laughter trailed behind her as he drew her close.

Damen's eyes narrowed as he watched Stephanie dance. Not traditional dancing now. The music was modern, the moves unchoreographed, and it was hard to see her for the other dancers thronging the outdoor dance space. But he glimpsed turquoise silk, that collar of crystals around her throat, bouncing curls and her glorious, uninhibited smile. A smile she never turned his way. Not since what had happened in Melbourne.

His throat dried to sandpaper roughness. He'd returned to the guest house to find her dressed for the wedding. She wore a dress once more in a style that left her arms and shoulders bare, the fabric attached around the neck only by that glinting collar. And when she turned the upper half of her back was tantalisingly bare.

Damen's palms had prickled with the urge to touch that expanse of skin. Or trace the gleaming fabric as it clung and dipped across her curves before flirting out around her legs. It was a dress made to drive a man to distraction.

She was made to drive him to distraction.

After a sleepless night he wasn't putting up much of a fight. All day he'd been on edge, his body hyper-alert as they acted the loving couple. As he leaned close to explain customs or conversations for her. As he endured the torture of Stephanie turning and murmuring to him, her breath an intimate caress.

Even entering the church and placing that gauzy wrap over her bare shoulders out of respect for tradition, only part of Damen's mind had been on the wedding or Manos or curious onlookers. Most of his brain had been cataloguing how very much he wanted Stephanie.

He'd held back, hadn't tried to seduce her in Manos's

home. Now he couldn't remember why that had seemed a point of honour.

She wanted him. He felt it in those tiny hitched sighs of hers, her dazed look when he touched her and the fluttering pulse that betrayed her time and again.

Damen leaned back in his chair, half listening to the conversation about global markets, financial recovery and bad debts. He couldn't stalk across and claim Stephanie. No one would believe he was so besotted with his new woman that he needed to be with her all the time. It would only make Manos suspicious.

Then the dancers parted and there she was, smiling up at her partner, who'd closed the space between them. He leaned in, whispering something, and she laughed.

Damen sat up, catching the rich yet breathless sound as the music faded.

His jaw clenched. He knew the guy dancing with her. He fancied himself irresistible with his ingratiating smile and practised charm. Let him work his charm on someone else!

'Don't you think, Damen—?'

'Sorry, Manos. Let's talk about this later. Stephanie needs me.' He was already out of his seat, stalking towards the dance floor.

She needed him all right, to keep her safe from suave seducers. From men who looked at her in that sexy dress and wanted her out of it. As he did.

Damen kept his eyes on her as he detoured past the DJ, throwing out not a request but a terse command. A loud pop song, just starting, stopped abruptly, making heads turn.

Stephanie turned too, her gaze colliding with Damen's, as he paced towards her. Her mouth, those lips that drove him again and again to the edge of control, opened as if she couldn't catch her breath.

The first bars of a new tune poured through the evening air, soft, slow, resonant with longing.

Damen saw her swallow, the wide circlet of exquisite crystals around her throat catching the glow from fairy lights strung all about.

Then he was there, looking down at her.

'My dance.'

In his peripheral vision her partner shifted his weight, huffed as if to say something, then faded away.

Damen reached out and did what he'd wanted to do all day. He slid his arm right round her back, low across her waist, feeling the exquisite softness of naked flesh against his palm. He pulled her close, snug against his thighs, and took her hand. His breath eased out in satisfaction. Better. Much better.

'What's the matter? You think Manos won't believe in us if we spend half an hour apart?' Her voice was a hoarse croak that lacerated his control. He wanted to hear more of it, throaty and out of breath, calling his name, crying out for release.

'I'm rescuing you from a playboy who thinks he can se-duce my woman.' Damen registered the growl roughening his voice and didn't care. He'd had enough.

The familiar ballad swelled around them and they began dancing, circling, barely moving from the spot.

'Was that necessary? You know I'm not going to be se-duced.'

Oh, yes, you are.

For sitting there, watching Stephanie with another man, something inside Damen had snapped. Not his patience. Something more fundamental. He didn't want to think about it or give it a name. He was a pragmatist and he knew the time for resisting was over. That was all he'd let himself consider.

Damen hauled her closer, pleased when her body melted against his despite the stunned expression in those wide golden-brown eyes.

Oh, yes. There'd definitely be a seduction tonight. And it would be he, Damen Nicolaides, orchestrating it. Beginning now.

Steph felt as if she was floating as they strolled down the secluded path. The faint sound of music reached her. Damen said the revellers would continue partying into the early hours, but the bride and groom had left and there was no need to linger.

Steph would have liked to linger, swaying in Damen's arms under the canopy of vines and tiny lights. For the first time since their charade began she hadn't given a thought to the lie they lived, for there, in his arms, it hadn't felt like a lie.

She was no fool. She knew it was the romantic setting, the handsome partner, Damen's proprietorial manner, which should have annoyed her and instead made her insides turn stupidly mushy, that created the strange ambience. Plus her own heightened desire.

She sighed. It was time to shake off the romantic illusion. When they entered their guest suite and were away from prying eyes, the masquerade would end. She was nothing more to Damen than the woman he'd paid a fortune to pretend to be his girlfriend. And he...well, he'd still be too potently alluring for her peace of mind but he needn't know that.

There it was, coming into view at last. The retreat they'd share for one more night. Would she lie awake again, wondering how it would be to indulge in a fling? Imagining being with Damen, the only man who'd broken through her wall of caution, awakening her body to desire?

A large moon hung low over the sea and silvery light bathed the scene in magic, making it impossibly beautiful. Something caught in her chest.

'It's been a wonderful day. Thank you.' Steph made to

withdraw her hand from Damen's but he kept hold of her fingers as they stopped on the terrace.

'Thank *you*, Stephanie.' His low voice skated across her skin, drawing it tight. 'I hadn't expected to enjoy today as much as I did.'

She shrugged. It had been a lovely celebration with friendly people. Even Manos, whose fierce, dark eyes had glittered dangerously at first, had mellowed as the evening progressed. Last seen, he'd been laughing with a group of men who'd shed their jackets, rolled up their sleeves and huddled around a table, drinking brandy and talking earnestly.

Steph moved towards the door but Damen blocked her way.

'Damen?' His arm came round her, drawing her close, his other hand still holding hers.

Delight shivered through her and she stiffened. It was one thing to enjoy the illicit pleasure of being in his arms, knowing it was for show, but they were alone here.

'What is it? Can you see someone?' Were they being watched?

His head lowered and for a snatched moment she imagined his mouth covering hers, those wide shoulders curving around her.

But he didn't do that. He'd promised not to kiss her. He'd signed a contract.

That memory stiffened her spine, a reminder that this wasn't real, as his mouth settled near her ear. Yet her eyes fluttered shut as his breath feathered her skin.

'I can't see anyone. That doesn't mean we can't be seen.' He paused. 'Hold me, Stephanie.'

Steph blinked her eyes open, trying to decipher the curious note in his voice. It wasn't an order so much as a request. There was a yearning in that deep voice that—

She pressed her lips together. There was no yearning, just a man speaking softly so anyone near by wouldn't hear. Reluctantly, enjoying every centimetre of sensation and knowing she shouldn't, Steph slid her hands up his chest to clasp the back of his neck.

He felt so good. That warm, woodsy scent tickled her nostrils and she ran her fingers through his thick hair, scraping along his scalp, telling herself she was making this look real for a potential onlooker, ignoring the fierce hunger drilling down through her middle.

A sigh shuddered through him, and then she was trembling too as his mouth moved along her jaw and down her neck. They weren't kisses exactly. Just the brush of his lips as he whispered something in gravelly Greek beneath his breath. The sound carved a channel of need through her, leaving her wide open and gently aching.

'Damen, I think we should go inside.' Because she couldn't play pretend lovers any more. Not tonight. Not when she felt so...

'Excellent idea, *kopela mou.*'

Yet instead of stepping back, Damen took her by surprise, bending to scoop her into his arms. The world tilted. Steph had never been held like this. Her arms went round his neck, hanging tight lest he drop her.

But it wasn't falling she feared. Not really. It was the riot going on inside her body. The jumble of excitement and anticipation, even knowing this was for the benefit of some unseen watcher.

'Do you really think this is necess—?'

'I do. Absolutely necessary.' His voice was as taut as her stretched nerves.

He opened the door, holding her in his arms, and stepped inside. All the while Steph was bombarded with new sensations. The feeling of being in his arms, surrounded by him. The heat where their bodies pressed together. The fact she could hear his heartbeat if she let herself rest her head against him. The awareness of how close his mouth was.

Above all the almost wonderful, almost scary, sense of being totally reliant on his strength.

Steph waited but Damen didn't release her.

'Damen? I can stand. No one can see us.' The massive windows on the sea side spilled moonlight into the large space, but they were private from prying eyes.

Instead of putting her down, Damen firmed his hold.

'Maybe I don't want to,' he murmured. 'Maybe I've been wanting to hold you like this all night.'

Steph's heart jumped. 'Stop it. We're not playing parts now. You can drop the besotted act.'

'And if it's not an act?' Above her his mouth twisted into a hard smile that looked like a grimace.

'What are you saying, Damen? That you've spent the last few hours longing to hold me like this?' It was preposterous, yet Steph heard the wobble in her voice, as if she wanted to believe it.

'That too. But what I really long for is your mouth on mine.' She felt as well as heard his voice rumble up from his chest. 'Your kisses. Your lips have been driving me crazy. *You've* been driving me crazy. Not just today. For weeks.'

Suddenly she was shoving at his shoulders, wiggling her legs, trying to sit up, get down, till eventually he relented and lowered her to the floor.

She felt her shawl slip to the floor but didn't pick it up. Steph backed up a step, far enough to meet Damen's dark eyes. In the gloom they should have been impossible to read. Instead she felt a punch to the solar plexus when she deciphered his expression.

Yearning, that was what she saw, or imagined she saw. A yearning such as she felt.

Except that couldn't be.

'Stop it. We don't have an audience here. There's no need to keep up the act.'

Slowly he turned his head from side to side. 'It's no act. That part hasn't ever been an act with you, Stephanie.'

Her nape tightened and her hands anchored at her hips. 'It was in Melbourne. That time in the car—'

'When we kissed?' His mouth curled at one side into something too taut to be a smile. 'I didn't plan that, you know. But how could I resist when you were so lush and inviting and I'd been trying to keep my distance all week? When we kissed it was like spring after the longest winter. Like sunshine after frost.' He shook his head. 'No, that's not right. It was more like a volcano erupting out of the blue. As if the caldera at Santorini exploded again, turning everything lava-hot. Burning away the world.'

The image branded her, deep inside, in that place where she tried to hide her feelings. He was right. It had been just like that. For her. Not for him. He'd merely been using her weakness against her.

'What's wrong, Damen?' She turned her voice to steel. 'Are you bored? Is it so difficult to go a few weeks without a woman in your bed that you'd even turn to *me*?'

Pain blanketed her chest but she made herself face him. If he knew how she really felt about him she'd be lost.

If she'd expected her lashing accusation to provoke him she was disappointed. 'Actually, I'm very discerning about who I take to bed. I learned the hard way to be very, very choosy.'

The hard way? Steph frowned, wondering what he meant.

'So what am I? A challenge? The one woman who refuses to be seduced by your charm?'

He folded his arms and she wished she didn't notice the way the gesture accentuated the power of his upper body. 'Definitely a challenge, Stephanie. But that's a separate issue. I've wanted you since I met you. The only reason I didn't seduce you that night in Australia was because I had an obligation to find your friend Emma for Christo. And after that,' he lifted his arms wide, 'I'd hurt you. It wasn't the time.'

To her surprise Steph thought she saw shame or at least regret flicker across his face.

'And you think things are different now? Because you're paying me?'

'They're absolutely different, and not because I'm paying you.' He shook his head. 'I never have and never will pay for a woman in my bed. This, what's between us, has nothing to do with money.'

Steph folded her arms across her chest, holding in her madly pounding heart.

'Then what's changed?'

'*You've* changed.' His night-dark eyes pinioned her. 'You've lost that wounded look as if I'm the big, bad wolf. Instead you look at me the way a woman does when she wants a man.'

Steph's chest rose hard on a shocked intake of air.

'You don't deny it.' His voice was soft as a summer breeze, warm as seduction.

'I don't need to deny it. You're paying me a fortune to pretend to be your lover. Of course I look at you…fondly. I have to be convincing.'

'Fondly?' Slowly he shook his head. 'It's more than that. You're not that good an actress.'

Steph's chin shot high. 'You've got an ego the size of the Aegean, Damen Nicolaides.'

'It's not ego, Stephanie. It's facing the truth. The same truth I faced ages ago. I *want* you, Stephanie, and I've given up pretending not to. You want me too.'

'In your dreams.'

'At least in my dreams I get to have you, Stephanie. There you're always willing and eager in my arms.'

Heat saturated her from the crown of her head to the soles of her feet. He dreamt of her? Just as she dreamt of him? Had he lain awake last night too, imagining what it would be like if they shared that big bed looking out over the sea?

'Nothing to say, Stephanie?'

She opened her mouth then shut it. Bandying words with him was too dangerous. Every word he spoke tapped into the secret channel of desire within her that she'd tried and failed to dam.

Damen stepped closer and her chin rose as she held his stare.

'You don't get anything in this life playing safe, Stephanie.'

'But you don't get burned either.' She hadn't planned to answer but then the words were out, revealing things she'd tried to hide. The yearning. The combustible heat within. The weakness.

Yet, instead of triumph, Damen's expression held understanding.

'Sometimes,' he murmured, 'playing with fire has compensations.'

He paused, watching her. Stephanie almost wished he'd reach for her, touch her and make the doubts disappear. Make it simple by stripping away her defences. But he didn't. He met her gaze gravely, not trying to hide his hunger. Not trying to hide anything. The silvery moonlight revealed features stark with longing but not a man who'd try to force her.

'If you're brave enough to take the risk.'

Steph tried to summon outrage, to be annoyed that he thought her a coward, just for being sensible. It didn't work because the pressure didn't come from Damen. It came from inside herself.

All her life Steph had played safe. Working, saving, planning for the future. Keeping herself to herself rather than venture into the wild realms of passion as so many of her peers had done. There'd been no boyfriends, no lovers. Just a man who'd duped her into trusting him, only to steal from her. And now Damen, who turned her inside out so she hardly recognised herself or what she felt.

She'd tried safety and it hadn't worked.

What did she have to lose?

As the thought surfaced the voice of reason screeched inside her brain, listing all the reasons this was dangerous.

For once Steph ignored the voice of reason.

'There's something I want.' Her voice held a strange, flat note, as if her heart weren't racing or her breaths coming in short gasps.

'Anything I can help with?' He didn't move but somehow he seemed nearer, the air thickening between them.

Steph unfolded her arms and let them hang by her sides. 'I'd like you to kiss me. On the lips.'

CHAPTER EIGHT

DAMEN'S BREATH SEARED IN, leaving his lungs overfull yet somehow without enough air to sustain him.

This was what he wanted. What he'd planned to get for so long. Yet, as he looked into Stephanie's serious face with that tiny frown on her brow and lips parted as if she too couldn't get enough oxygen, it wasn't triumph he felt. Or not entirely.

The hammer beat in his blood revealed the depth of his need. He wasn't besting her. This wasn't a contest. He felt almost scared to touch her, as if she'd melt away or change her mind and he'd be left alone, the craving for her eating him up.

Damen didn't let himself hesitate. He stepped in to stand toe to toe with her. Her nipples grazed him and a spiral of hot metal coiled down from his chest to his groin, screwing his body tighter and hotter.

He palmed her bare back. Her flesh was velvety. His other hand ploughed through her curls, tilting her head. She looked up at him with wide, wary eyes. It was too dark to see their golden depths but even in the gloom he felt her scrutiny. As if she didn't trust him to make this worth her while. As if expecting him to let her down.

That spurred him to take his time, though he wanted to plunder her lips till she stopped thinking and gave him everything.

He pressed his lips to the corner of her mouth, teasing them both, telling himself he could withstand a few more moments' waiting. She trembled and something hard inside softened.

Damen gentled his hand on her scalp, slid his mouth along her cheek, peppering tiny kisses along flesh that tasted like vanilla and something far more precious. To the edge of her jawline, to her ear. Slender fingers grabbed his upper arms. He felt rather than heard her sigh.

That was when his patience disintegrated, even as he told himself to go slow. Now he was back at her mouth, tugging her bottom lip between his teeth, hearing her gasp, feeling her fingers dig into his flesh through his jacket. Damen licked that delicate lower lip, savouring a taste of paradise.

He was telling himself to move on, press more teasing kisses along her jawline, when Stephanie slicked her tongue along the seam of his mouth. A second later she fastened her teeth on his bottom lip and nipped hard.

Sensations, raw and hot, shot through him. All thought of slow seduction faded as he gathered her in, hauling her against a body forged hard as steel.

No coaxing now, just a driving hunger that melded their lips, their tongues tangling in a wild dance of eager ecstasy.

Stephanie quivered against him, but not with nerves. Not with her hands clutching so tight it was as if she wanted to climb up him, all the better to devour him. And even though he, from his superior height, bowed her back over his arm, this wasn't about dominance and submission.

Submission! She was anything but submissive. She didn't just kiss with her lips but with her whole, glorious body. She undulated against him, a symphony of female sensuality as her tongue danced in his mouth, eager and erotic.

Still it wasn't enough. The kiss was deep and druggingly arousing, yet he needed more. With a grunt Damen tugged her closer against his arousal. His arm at her waist shifted till he grasped her bottom and lifted her.

Shards of heat shot through him. It wasn't enough. Not with the taste of Stephanie like sweet, wild honey in his mouth and the feel of her eager body against him.

Damen heard a hum of sound, a low, vibrating growl. It took a moment to realise it came from him. A gruff sound of encouragement and demand so primal it startled him.

Nothing about this kiss was ordinary. He'd expected pleasure, anticipated arousal. He'd even spoken to her of volcanic heat, yet till their mouths touched he'd forgotten how devastating it was, kissing Stephanie Logan.

This was elemental. Like a combustible chemical reaction and as inevitable as the sun rising tomorrow.

Damen gave himself up to it, letting the relentless driving force take him, knowing that to resist, even to think, was pointless.

Some time later, he had no idea how much later, he lifted his head enough to allow them both to breathe. His lungs worked like bellows and his brain had ceased functioning beyond *mine, mine, mine.*

He blinked, trying to ground himself, stunned at his loss of control. At his inability to think. As if he were the one out of his depth.

Damen looked into slumberous eyes slowly opening to look up at him, at a kiss-ravaged mouth, those lips plump and pouting, and self-knowledge smote him. He *was* reeling. For the first time he wasn't in command of himself.

He didn't give a damn.

He wanted more. He wanted everything.

Her hand on his chest stopped him when he made to kiss her again.

'Wait. Stop.'

Chest heaving, Damen paused.

'Yes?'

'This feels dangerous.'

Damen suppressed a smile. 'Not dangerous, *agapi mou.* Just a little on the edge.'

Who was he kidding? They were combustible. It was like saying a summer wildfire, scorching all before it, was just a little dangerous.

'I can't think when we kiss.' Her voice was breathless, wondering, and Damen wanted to reassure her everything was okay. That she could rely on him to put the brakes on.

But he couldn't. Kissing Stephanie was like being on a runaway train and never wanting to get off.

He shook his head and straightened. 'You're right. When we kiss…'

He paused, cleared his throat. The man he'd become didn't admit to weakness. He'd forced himself to learn from his past, catastrophic mistake. He didn't hand anyone, especially a woman, the power of holding the truth about him.

It would be easy to step back, murmur something about respecting her desire for caution. Well, not easy, but more acceptable than admitting the truth, that she threatened to undo him.

'When we kiss?' Her eyes searched his, her hands still clutching his arms as if she needed his support to stay upright.

Damen could lie, brush off the truth and walk away. But if he did, would he ever hold her in his arms again? The thought of never kissing her again left him bereft.

'When we kiss,' he growled, 'I don't want to stop. I want you, Stephanie. Completely. Unreservedly. I want you wild, wanton and abandoned. I want to worship you with my body till you scream in ecstasy and barely have the energy to give yourself to me again. And I want to keep loving you till we're both wrung-out wrecks, unable to move.'

Damen's lips twisted into a grimace. So much for keeping the truth to himself. To not handing her power on a plate.

Steph felt the thrill of excitement start in her belly and spread in radiating waves. She trembled so hard surely Damen saw. Yet he scowled down at her as if she'd done something wrong.

He looked so *fierce*. As if he wanted to fight rather than kiss. As if this were some battle between them.

Slowly she processed his words. Not just the shiver-inducing promise of sexual satisfaction but that revealing comment. *I don't want to stop.*

Steph didn't pretend to be an expert about Damen but she knew some things about him. One was that he guarded himself. He thought before he acted, each action planned and scrutinised. He didn't rush headlong into things but considered them, then worked out the strategy that would best suit his needs, like hiring a faux-girlfriend.

He'd even taken a pragmatic approach to his love life, guarding against importunate lovers via his arrangement with Clio.

Yet there was nothing pragmatic about his expression now.

He looked different, his features stripped back as if passion had scoured any softness from his face. Yet Steph felt no fear, just fellow feeling. It was the same for her. As if their kiss had stolen away the comfortable platitudes she surrounded herself with and left only a single truth.

She wanted Damen, and no amount of prevaricating or pretending could change that.

Beneath her palm his heart thundered.

They were equals in this. He'd admitted as much. It wouldn't be safe. It would be wild and ecstatic. But maybe just once in her life she should discover what that felt like. Step off the straight and narrow and let herself go.

It wasn't as if Damen would be around long term, interfering with her life or trying to turn a moment's wildness into something more significant.

The choice was hers.

Steph moistened her lips, aware of Damen's eyes following the movement. It sent a corkscrew of heat twisting through her.

'I'm not experienced.'

His head reared back as if he needed to distance himself and Steph felt a jerk of dismay at that tiny withdrawal. Damen blinked, his eyes narrowing as if wondering if he'd heard right.

'Not *very* experienced?'

Was this a deal-breaker for him? Pride told her if her virginity was a problem, then tough, he'd be the one to miss out. But she wanted him so badly. Couldn't imagine turning back now.

Her chin rose and she focused on a point beyond his shoulder. 'It doesn't matter. Forget I spoke.'

Warm fingers cupped her chin and turned her face to his. 'It matters, *kopela mou*.' He breathed deep, his chest a living wall before her. 'Thank you for telling me.' He paused. 'It's an unexpected…responsibility.'

She opened her mouth to say it wasn't a responsibility, just a physical fact she thought he should know about. But before she could speak his mouth covered hers.

This kiss was different. Not desperate or wild. It was light, gentle, but with no less purpose and no less pleasure. It was a kiss that tasted sweet with promise, heady with longing and as it went on something vital melted inside her. Steph could almost swear she heard music somewhere, beautiful music. But that was impossible.

Heat rose, weaving through her blood, softening her bones. Steph leaned into him, needing his strength to support her, and once more Damen scooped her close.

This time when he lifted his head, breathing hard through his nostrils, there was no looking away, no pretending. He stared down at her and it felt as though he saw her in a way no one else ever had. It should have been scary but it felt right. Steph wanted him to see her, the real her, to be as wholly caught up in this moment as she was.

Damen lifted his fingers to her forehead, smoothing a line above her eyebrows. 'There's nothing to worry about, Stephanie. I promise you.'

She wasn't worried. Well, not much. But there was no need for words as Damen led her to the bed.

'Undress me.' His voice, low as a caress, wound through her as he shrugged out of his jacket and tossed it over a chair. His shoulders looked so broad in that white shirt, gleaming in the moonlight. Her fingers twitched and she swallowed hard, knowing she'd fumble her way through undressing him, revealing her ineptitude and nervous excitement.

What did it matter?

Steph reached for his bow tie, the silk soft to the touch as he undid his cufflinks. Tugging the tie free, she undid the top of his shirt then got distracted by the dark, silky skin she revealed. The pads of her fingers slid across his collarbone, discovering dips and notches, then down to where a smattering of crisp hair dusted his chest. It tickled her fingers and palms when she spread them across that wall of hot muscle.

One brown nipple budded under her palm and Damen's skin tightened as muscles jumped then eased.

Steph looked up to find his gaze fixed, dark and glowing on her as he reefed off his shirt. His hands went to his belt and the thrumming beat of her heart rose to her throat.

Her hands drifted lower, discovering flesh that was surprisingly soft, taut over muscle and bone. Her gaze followed her hands and she discovered he'd shucked his trousers and underwear down to his ankles, standing before her proudly erect.

Steph's throat tightened. He looked impossibly beautiful, impossibly huge. A flutter of nerves butterflied through her middle to settle between her legs, turning into a hot, achy sensation that made her shift restlessly.

Damen said nothing, just stood with his arms at his sides, waiting.

Steph anchored one palm on that flat abdomen and dragged her other down, fingertips touching the thatch of dark hair then reaching his heavy arousal. To her surprise it felt like silk over solid heat. Tentatively she curled her hand around him, sliding gently right to the tip.

A sound like the wind soughing through trees penetrated the silence. It took a moment to realise it was Damen, sighing in pleasure, his eyes glittering through narrowed slits.

She repeated the movement, feeling a rising power, and this time he moved, thrusting into her hand, his hips tilting to follow her caress.

'You like that.' It should have sounded stupid. It probably did sound naïve. Yet Damen didn't laugh. The tendons in his neck stood proud and the muscles in his arms and chest bunched as if he forced himself into immobility.

'I do. When you touch me I feel…' He shook his head, his mouth a grimace as Steph let her other hand dance, feather light across his abdomen, grazing one hip, then down, then up again.

She saw what it cost him to stand while she looked her fill, exploring. She watched his pulse judder, saw the sheen at his throat as if he was burning up. Damen was a strong man, used to wielding authority, making things happen. Yet he held himself still, giving her time to adjust. Giving her power.

Because she'd told him she was inexperienced. Because he knew she was nervous as well as excited. Suddenly she wasn't nervous any more. Not enough to wait, at any rate.

She dropped to her knees before him, scrabbling to find first one gleaming shoe then another, helping him out of them and his socks till he could step free of his clothes and stand naked before her. She lifted her eyes, drawn once more by the uncompromising shape of his erection. Would he—?

Damen's hand closed around hers, drawing her up.

He didn't say anything, simply reached around to the back of the halter-neck collar of her dress and flicked it undone. Steph blinked, her arm automatically lifting to hold the bodice up while Damen dragged the side zipper open. Then his arms dropped and he stood, waiting.

Steph's heart thundered as she released the fabric, felt it slide free, down her breasts, stomach and thighs, to land with a plop around her feet.

Damen's chest rose mightily then sank again before he lifted one hand, brushing across her breasts. He teased her nipples with a barely there touch that sent shocking jolts of heat shooting to that needy place between her legs.

'And your shoes.' His voice was a whisper of sound, barely audible over her pulse.

Steph reached for his arm, clutched as she lifted one foot and fumbled at the buckle, drawing off the high heel. Then the other. Now she stood before him, naked but for panties of skimpy lace.

She drew a deep breath, registering a new scent in the air, not the evocative scent she associated with Damen but something headier, slightly musky.

Arousal. That was what she smelt in the air thickening between them. It was what she felt pounding through her blood, heating her body till she glowed.

Eyes on Damen's, she hooked her thumbs under the lace at her hips and dragged it down, letting it pool at her feet.

His gaze tracked down, zeroing in on the dark V between her legs, and his mouth crooked up at one side as if in approval. He lifted his hand, palm up, and Steph put hers in it, feeling relief and excitement as his fingers folded around hers. Fire skated from their linked hands all the way up her arm then down, down, deep inside. He led her to the bed, drawing her down beside him so they sat side by side.

It wasn't what she'd expected. She'd supposed that once naked they'd be in each other's arms, kissing, letting nature take its course in a flurry of urgent excitement.

Instead the line of Damen's jaw looked almost grim in the spill of moonlight.

'I want to make this good for you, Stephanie. You'll need to tell me what you like and what you don't.'

'I don't know.' Steph swallowed, feeling suddenly gauche.

Damen shook his head. 'You will soon enough. Promise me,' he paused, 'if you feel uncomfortable, tell me and I'll stop. At any point. Agreed?'

She nodded, suddenly alarmed at the possibility he might

expect more than she knew how to give. She thought of stories she'd heard about sexual kinks and—

'Don't worry, *koritsi mou*. All you have to do is enjoy yourself. Okay?'

Steph nodded. She hated feeling like this, with no clue. So she lifted her palm to his shoulder, feeling a frisson of response in the shiver that passed through his big frame.

'What I'd really like,' she said, her voice hoarse, 'is to kiss you. To lie against you naked and kiss you.'

The serious expression around his eyes eased and the smile he sent her was pure devilry. 'Since you insist.'

Then, before she had a chance to register movement, she was flat on her back on the mattress, with Damen lying half above, half beside her, his shoulders wide against the streaming moonlight.

Steph sucked in an urgent breath, full of that heady scent of Damen and sex. It lifted her breasts against his chest and everything inside stopped for a second in sheer wonder at how good that felt. But there was more, far more. The scratchy friction of his hairy leg, hot as it slid over hers. Hard fingers pushing through her hair, holding her still as his mouth lowered to hers.

This time his kiss stole her breath instantly. For they were together as never before. So close, touching everywhere. The furnace-like heat of his tall frame, even the way his arms caged her as he propped himself above her, taking some of his weight, all added to the amazing intimacy.

Soon that expectant stillness vanished, obliterated by the need for more of what Damen gave her. His hard body against hers, his hands moving knowingly, his mouth... Oh, his mouth. That earlier kiss had been a mere prelude to what he did now, drawing her to the edge of ecstasy with his mouth on hers till she writhed, eager for more.

Strong hands clamped hers, lifting her arms above her head.

'What—?'

'It's okay. We just need to slow things a little. I don't have many condoms with me and they need to last the night.' He nipped the sensitive place between her neck and shoulder, making her gasp.

'That's not slowing things. That's...' Her words ended with a sigh as Damen worked his way up to her ear, kissing, nipping, turning her to jelly. Yet before she could catch her breath he moved down her body, settling between her thighs as if he belonged there and capturing her breasts in his hands. His breath was hot on first one nipple then the other as he blew across them, watching them rise to aching points.

'Please, Damen.'

He lifted his head. 'You don't like this?'

Steph shook her head. 'I do. Too much.'

'Then relax, and I'll show you how much better it can be.'

That was the start of what she thought of later as exquisite torture. Damen worked his way around her body, drawing wild responses from the tiniest caresses. And all the time she heard his voice, deep enough to shudder through her bones, asking if she liked this, or this. When the truth was she liked it all. Too much. Each new caress, each press of his lips or stroke of his hand drew the tension in her tighter.

Till finally, with a gleam in his dark eyes, he sank once more between her thighs. It took just the touch of his tongue, a single, sliding stroke, and Steph shattered in a piercing explosion of pleasure. Light burst in a rainbow of colour behind her eyelids, the breath seized in her lungs and her body stretched taut, racked by aftershocks that gradually diminished, leaving her dazed and boneless.

Finally she opened her eyes. There was Damen, his gaze fixed on her, his face intent, as if there was nothing more important than her pleasure.

Steph's mouth curled up in a breathless smile. 'Before you ask, I *did* like that.'

His answering grin was the sexiest thing she'd seen, perhaps because of where he lay, his broad shoulders between
the V of her legs.

'Good. Let's do it again.'

Steph lifted herself on one elbow, a protest forming on
her lips because of course she couldn't possibly climax like
that again, not now she was totally sated.

Except it seemed Damen knew her better than she did.
This time he used tongue, lips and teeth to ease her back into
that state of frantic need, while his long fingers explored and
delved, making her arch off the bed as that tightness gathered again, sensitive nerve endings singing with excitement.

All through it, Damen held her gaze.

That, his knowing look, the dark, hungry gleam that ca-
ressed as surely as his hand and mouth, was what turned her
to mush. Stopped the protest that had formed in her mouth.
Why would she want to stop anything that felt so wonderful?

That time when she came Steph screamed, her fingers
clutching the thick hair on Damen's head, her eyes locked
with his. Her cries took ages to die, morphing into something like a sob as finally he prowled his way up her body
and she could put her arms around him, clutching him close.

She squeezed him tight, wrapping her leaden legs around
him, burrowing her face into his shoulder, drawing the spicy
hot scent of him deep inside. In the pulsing quiet everything seemed to slow and centre. Steph felt as if she'd discovered a new world, a place she'd never known existed.
Because of Damen.

Eventually there was movement as he rolled over, taking her with him so she lay straddled and boneless across
his tall frame.

For a long time they lay like that, unmoving, till finally
Damen stroked his hand down Steph's spine and, to her
surprise, she felt herself arch into him.

'Are you ready for more, Stephanie?'

'More?' Blearily she lifted her head but his meaning

was clear as he shifted and she felt the slide of his arousal against her core.

Of course there was more. He'd given her orgasms and it was only fair he should claim his own. Yet as his hips tilted and Steph felt the press of that iron and silk shaft between her legs, she didn't feel as exhausted as she had before. Instead she was…excited. Her breath caught deep in her chest as Damen's hands brushed her breasts, then sank to her hips.

Experimentally Steph slid against him and was shocked by the white-hot bolt of heat that shot through her.

'I like that,' he growled, his voice barely recognisable. The sound of it, rough and hungry, made something dance inside, some feminine part of her that revelled in the idea of Damen on the edge. 'Do you?'

For answer Steph moved again, more deliberately, bracing her hands on his shoulders, concentrating on his flesh gliding against hers. 'I do.'

In the gloom she caught his grin, or was it a grimace? 'Good. Then take me.'

It took Steph a moment to digest his meaning. It wasn't what she'd expected. She'd imagined him propped over her, powering into her, setting their rhythm.

But this was the man who'd taken an age pleasuring her, leashing his own desires to make her first time good. More than good. The wetness between her legs, the melting sensation there, told its own story. Now he let her set the pace. How much easier could he have made it? If there was going to be pain, she sensed it would be fleeting.

Besides, she decided as she wriggled back a little, despite her climaxes, Damen had left her with an aching emptiness inside. An emptiness she wanted him to fill.

She rose onto her knees then gingerly reached for him, finding him already sheathed. His fingers clamped tighter around her hips.

'Like this?' She centred herself over him, watching him nod, seeing his mouth pull back into a flat line as she slowly sank. It was the weirdest feeling, a stretching sensation that made her pause, panting.

Steph waited for him to tell her to keep going, to pull her down with those large hands, but he simply waited, watching, till the slight discomfort faded. She tilted her hips and, as if in response, Damen lifted up from beneath in a long, slow glide that stole her breath.

'More,' he urged in a voice of gravel.

Steph blinked. There was more? How was that possible?

She longed to find out. Steadying herself on his shoulders, she bore down till they were locked together with him buried deep inside.

She blinked, astonished at how easy it had been and how remarkable it felt. Except Damen's hands on her hips were urging her up. She followed the prompting, then blinked as he tugged her back down while he tilted his pelvis and thrust.

The sensation was amazing. It felt...

Steph gasped a shocked breath and repeated the movement, more smoothly this time, meeting the angle of his thrust with her own, then feeling the aftershock ripple through her like the shadow of an earthquake.

'Damen. Please, I...'

Her body began to shake, those worn-out muscles trembling as pleasure rose. Not like before. This was bigger, deeper, tugging at her soul as well as her body. She felt them moving as one, then moving in counterpoint, making the most remarkable magic between them.

That was how it felt. Magic.

Like the most profound magic in the world. Steph felt bigger than herself, part of something wondrous.

Maybe it was the way Damen held her eyes as they made the magic together, or the press of his hands so possessive at her hips. The thrusting caress of his body within hers, circling in a way that shot showers of flaming sparks through the darkness at the edge of her vision.

Then she heard it, Damen's voice, but not his voice. A low growl of triumph and wonder as he called her name and thrust high. Suddenly she was falling to meet him, the whole world bursting into flames around her, consuming her, cradling her in a fiery embrace that became Damen's embrace, his arms tight round her, his breath caressing her cheek, holding her to him as ecstasy took them both.

CHAPTER NINE

DAMEN WATCHED HER SLEEPING. It had been late when finally they'd collapsed, sated, in a tangle on the sheets. For hours after that he'd lain there, unable to sleep, his brain racing as he surveyed the woman curled so trustingly in his arms.

He didn't do post-coital cuddles. He didn't invite lovers to spend the night. Not in ten years. Not since Ingrid.

He waited for the familiar shudder of revulsion at the name but for once it didn't come. Probably because he held Stephanie warm and limp in his embrace.

Last night had felt like a turning point and he'd spent the last couple of hours inventing plausible reasons for that.

Because she'd been a virgin.

Because he'd wanted her for so long, longer than he'd ever wanted and gone without a woman.

Because, although he'd paid for her presence in his world, she'd made it clear that she gave her body as a gift that had nothing to do with the contract they'd negotiated or the masquerade they played.

Because her innocence and forthrightness were a combination so heady it made her different to any other woman he'd let into his life.

Because he'd *let* her into his life. He'd explained the reasons for their masquerade, explained his relationship with Manos and Clio, he who never explained himself to any woman.

He sensed that last came closest to the truth.

Damen had let Stephanie in, not just to his bed, but under his guard in ways that hadn't been apparent till too late.

Now, watching the sun rise over the Aegean, the pink and apricot dawn light changing to a clear blue sky, Damen wasn't concentrating on the work he'd do later from his yacht, or the discussions he'd have with Manos. He was thinking about how and when he'd have Stephanie again. Whether she'd be sore from making love and whether he should back off for a day and whether he had the resolve to do that if she needed space. Whether she'd enjoy it if he took her from behind, and how she'd feel about spending the whole day naked in his bed.

He scrubbed his palm over his face, trying to erase the erotic fantasies that crowded his brain.

Every time he tried to think about the next few weeks, even the next couple of days, he circled back to Stephanie naked beneath him, above him, before him. Stephanie caressing him. How would she feel about using her mouth on him?

She sighed and stretched voluptuously, her lips soft against his chest, her legs sliding around his, sending his temperature soaring and his libido into overdrive.

Damen waited, breathless, for her to wake. Instead she sank more deeply against him as if he were her own private pillow. Her even breathing was a caress against sensitised flesh. The sight of her pink nipple, trembling invitingly with each rise of her chest, was designed, surely, to taunt him.

Carefully Damen slid from the bed, propping a pillow under her arm and cheek, telling himself he didn't really want her to wake. Because Stephanie would wake full of questions.

Questions he had no desire to answer.

Questions about how their relationship would change now they were lovers.

Loping to the wardrobe, Damen gritted his teeth. The answer was simple. There was no change. Not in any material way. They'd go on as before except—here he allowed himself a satisfied smile—that when they were alone they could indulge their taste for passion. He was pretty sure after last night that Stephanie, so sensual and passionate, would be eager for that.

But that would be only in the privacy of their bed. Nothing else was different. She wasn't his girlfriend. There'd be no long-term relationship, no matter how phenomenal the sex.

Damen grabbed swim shorts and a towel. He'd take an early dip and give her some privacy when she woke. She'd appreciate that.

And it would signal that nothing significant had altered. She was smart. She'd understand he wouldn't make promises he had no intention of keeping. Promises that might lead a woman to believe in happy endings.

No fear of that with Stephanie, despite the surprise of her virginity. She was here solely for the money. She'd made no bones about that. She wouldn't start dreaming of a wedding ring just because they'd enjoyed sex.

Which meant, he realised as he dragged the shorts on, that she really was the perfect woman. Sexy, passionate and short-term.

Damen smiled and let himself out into the sunshine. It was going to be a glorious day.

Where was she?

Damen stalked along the path to the main house, his brow knotted as he scanned the terrace where last night guests had danced till late. It was empty and tidy too, as if an army of helpers had cleared away last night's detritus.

She must be here. There was no other possibility.

When he'd returned to the guest house it had been empty, the bed tidy, Stephanie's bag packed beside it. But there'd been no sign of her. Only the lingering aroma of coffee in the air, making his nostrils twitch.

Damen had returned warily. He'd enjoyed his morning swim, then, since it was early, had swum to the *Amphitrite* to put in an hour's work on the computer. An hour had become two but he'd known Stephanie would be exhausted after last night. *He'd* been exhausted, but so energised with his brain on overload, rest had been out of the question.

Besides, he admitted to a lingering doubt about whether she'd see their situation with quite the same clarity he did. Women could be emotional and it would be no surprise if, the morning after losing her virginity, Stephanie was a little clingy.

He should never have had sex with her, not after discovering she was still innocent, sexually at least. But abstinence had been impossible by the time he'd tasted her lips.

He'd returned to the guest house wondering if he approached an emotional battleground.

Only to find that, far from clinging unbearably, Stephanie had deserted him!

Pain arced through his jaw and he realised he was grinding his teeth.

He didn't want her clinging but he didn't expect her to disappear. What if he'd wanted to discuss this development in their relationship? What about laying out new ground rules? Had she no consideration?

He pushed open the door to Manos's home and followed the sound of voices.

Steph looked up from the laptop as Clio offered another plate of goodies. Baklava this time, dripping with sweet syrup. 'Truly, I couldn't eat any more.'

'Nonsense. You worked hard helping out, which you shouldn't have done, being a visitor.'

'I was glad to help. It was nice to be involved.'

She'd arrived at the big house to find Clio, her mother and Damen's mother putting things to rights after the caterers had finished the heavy work of clearing up.

It had been a relief to see Clio's warm smile, and accept her offer of breakfast with the three women in the massive kitchen.

Steph had felt so very alone this morning.

She'd told herself she was being overly emotional. Of course she hadn't expected Damen to be there, waiting to share breakfast with her.

Or hold her in his arms as he'd done last night.

She'd woken to unaccustomed aches in places she'd never ached. Not badly, just a gentle throb that reminded her of how they'd spent the night.

It was stupid to want those strong arms holding her close to the comforting thud of Damen's heart. Stupid to long for his hoarse endearments in Greek that melted her insides, for that sense of oneness that had transformed a physical act into something wondrous.

Steph should be grateful he'd left early and she'd had the guest house to herself. There'd been no stilted morning-after conversation. She'd been able to take a leisurely bath and make strong, sweet coffee to help banish the lingering wisps of fantasy.

Because it had been fantasy. A night of glorious passion in the arms of her perfect lover.

But now it was a new day. The passion was gone and so was her lover. Damen wasn't perfect and nor was she. She'd made the massive mistake of giving in to desire, telling herself she could enjoy simple sex then walk away.

Now she realised there was no such thing as simple sex. Not for her, and not with Damen.

'Try it at least,' Clio urged. 'Mama made it to a family recipe.'

Steph took a spoonful and glorious flavours exploded in her mouth. 'This is stunning.'

From the other side of the kitchen Clio's mother beamed. 'I'm glad you like it. It's the least I can do, especially as you're doing me this big favour.' She nodded to the laptop in front of Steph on the marble island bench. 'If I can get away for a little while, maybe even persuade Manos...' She shrugged. 'You have no idea how much that would mean.'

Steph looked at the worry lines marking the older woman's face and remembered Manos's dark eyes flashing with suppressed temper yesterday. Damen had said Manos would make his whole family's life miserable if he didn't get his way. It seemed he'd been doing just that. Even beautiful Clio looked tired and drawn.

Suddenly Steph was glad she'd agreed to Damen's scheme to rescue Clio from her father's machinations.

But she could do more. 'I think I've got the perfect place for the quiet holiday you wanted. It's in a scenic part of Italy, not crowded with tourists yet gorgeous and utterly peaceful. I found it for clients recently and they loved it.' She turned the laptop.

'Is that a convent?' The women crowded close.

'Yes, but the accommodation is luxurious. It's a guest house in the grounds and no tourists are allowed, only the nuns and their guests. There are views to the lake and mountains plus a walled courtyard full of roses.' Steph scrolled through photos, pleased to see her audience's excitement. 'It's a short walk to town, where there are restaurants and a supermarket if you want to self-cater.' Manos might be wealthy but his wife enjoyed cooking.

'The comforts of home,' Clio murmured, 'without the stresses.'

Her mother nodded. 'It looks amazing. How did you know about it?'

'It's what I do. I'm a travel advisor and I specialise…specialised in tailoring unique holiday experiences. Mainly at the luxury end of the market.'

'Specialised, past tense?' Clio asked as the two older women focused on the photos. 'What happened?'

Steph shrugged. 'It's a tough time in the travel industry. Lots of people don't think they need professional help when they can trawl the internet themselves.'

Clio tilted her head, as if considering. 'But if you were working at the luxury end of the market…?'

Steph met her questioning gaze and finally nodded. It

wasn't a secret really, even if she didn't usually like discussing it. 'I came unstuck in a business venture.'

'Oh, rotten luck. The business model wasn't sound?'

Steph knew Clio was running her own start-up company and didn't take offence at her direct question. 'Oh, it was sound. Sadly my partner wasn't.'

She turned as Manos and Damen entered the kitchen, Manos speaking Greek and gesturing emphatically.

Steph's skin prickled as she met Damen's unblinking green stare.

Last time he'd seen her they'd been naked in bed.

She sat straighter, wishing she had more than palazzo pants and a slinky top to keep her safe from that heated gaze. He only had to look at her and her skin heated to a fiery blush.

Could everyone tell? Did they all know that she and he…?

Belatedly she stopped her runaway thoughts. Of course no one else knew she'd given Damen her virginity last night. Or that she'd spent hours learning how dangerous a patient, generous, potently desirable man could be to her equilibrium. As far as the world was concerned, she and Damen were already lovers, even if Clio suspected otherwise.

Steph drew a breath and tried to tame her racing pulse. She nodded to both men. 'Good morning. Have you come to join us for coffee?'

The morning tested Damen's patience.

He wanted, desperately, to get Stephanie alone. He'd told himself he needed to clarify with her that nothing had changed, that she had no expectations beyond their contract. Yet to his chagrin it seemed there was no need. She treated him with a casual friendliness that should have pleased him, yet instead irked.

Or maybe he wanted to get her alone so they could revisit some of last night's more spectacular moments. Since waking he'd been unable to concentrate fully on anything but the memory of her satiny skin, her sighs of pleasure and the exquisite delight she'd offered him.

But every attempt to be alone with her was thwarted. By Clio and her mother offering food and coffee. By Manos, eager to talk business. By the interested gleam in his own mother's eyes as she looked from Damen to Stephanie and back again, clearly wondering if there was more to their relationship than he'd let on.

Obviously he wasn't the only one to notice Stephanie's delightful blush when their eyes met. It was the only hint that anything had changed between them.

Such as him taking her virginity in the night.

That knowledge throbbed through him every time he saw her looking cool and exasperatingly sexy in jade-green silk and those wide, floaty trousers that made him think of veils and beds and sex.

Damen considered himself a modern man, not hung up on old traditions. Yet to his surprise, the knowledge he'd been Stephanie's first lover branded itself on his psyche. He felt...engaged. Protective. Possessive.

He wanted to haul her away to somewhere private where he could keep her for himself.

Which didn't make sense when he'd already told himself nothing had altered between them.

By the time they finally finished their goodbyes, late in the afternoon, and headed for the yacht, Damen's patience hung by a thread.

He should have been pleased that Stephanie didn't attempt to talk on the walk to the beach, or the short trip to the yacht. There were no fluttering eyelashes, no hand on his arm as she leaned close to whisper in his ear. None of the tactics previous lovers had used to manufacture an illusion of emotional intimacy. Instead she seemed interested in everything but him. The colour of the water. The view of the island. The silver flash as a school of fish passed them. Even her phone, as if she had urgent business to conduct.

Which reminded him. Her partner. Who was that? He'd caught the phrase as he walked into the kitchen. He'd been listening to Manos but, as usual, when Stephanie was near, Damen's attention veered straight to her.

Who was this partner? He couldn't have been a lover, since only Damen could claim that role. Yet dissatisfaction niggled. He needed to know more.

When they stepped onto the deck Damen took Stephanie's arm and guided her into the privacy of a sitting room. For an instant she looked as if she'd protest, but only for an instant. She must realise there was no point trying to avoid this discussion.

He waited till the door was closed and Stephanie stood by the window, as if drawn to the view of the island.

Damen was drawn to the view of her. Utterly alluring despite the tight set of her shoulders. Was she going to make trouble after all?

'Are you okay?'

It wasn't what he'd planned to say. It surprised her too, for she swung to face him, eyes wide.

'Of course. Don't I look it?'

What she looked was sumptuously inviting. Her slender curves showed to advantage in that outfit and her skin had a healthy glow.

Was she embarrassed? Nervous under his scrutiny?

Her chin lifted and her eyebrows too, as if challenging him.

'You look fine.' Her eyes narrowed and he hurried on. 'More than fine.' Damen cursed his sudden inability to articulate. 'We need to talk.'

Did he imagine that Stephanie tensed? Her mouth drew into a flat line, as if she didn't want to hear what he had to say.

'Go on.'

Damen stuck his hands in the pockets of his jeans. Did he start by finding out how she felt physically after last night? Or come straight to the point and reiterate that their agreement hadn't changed?

He opened his mouth and heard himself say, 'Tell me about your partner.'

'Sorry?' She definitely stood straighter this time, arms curving around her waist in a defensive gesture.

So the guy *was* important to her. Damen had sensed it. 'Earlier today you said something about a partner. I want to know about him.'

'Why? He has nothing to do with this…us…' She made a wide, arcing gesture.

'I don't want any loose ends that might complicate things. We've still got six weeks together and I don't want any murky surprises.'

Steph bit her lip. Murky surprises. That was one way to describe Jared. He'd wrecked her life and even now she couldn't be rid of him. Not with Damen standing there like the lord of all he surveyed, demanding she lift the lid on her private life.

Disappointment was a swirling, bitter pool in her stomach.

What did she expect? That after last night Damen would turn to her with affection in his eyes? Or at least softness?

That he'd want to be alone with her to make love again? Because, like her, he felt bound together by this spell, even when they were surrounded by others?

Except it wasn't making love, it was sex.

Yet every time she'd met his eyes today she'd felt a great whump of emotion slam into her, like the roar of a bonfire igniting in a rush of flame. Heat trickled through her at the connection they shared, the connection no one else seemed to have noticed.

She was deluded. There was no connection. Last night

meant nothing to him. She wouldn't allow herself to be so pathetic as to reveal how much it had meant to her.

'You needn't worry. He's out of my life. I'll never see him again.'

'Nevertheless, I need to know.' He paused, expectant. Finally he added, 'I'll treat what you tell me in confidence. I just need to know nothing from your past will derail our... arrangement.'

Clearly her word wasn't good enough.

Steph bit back the words of hurt cramming onto her tongue.

But a look at Damen's set jaw and hard eyes told her he wouldn't back down. Besides, what did it matter? She was past the stage of caring what he thought of her gullibility. She'd laid herself wide open to him last night, not just physically, but emotionally too, and he didn't give a damn. There'd been no tenderness today, no acknowledgement. Nothing.

It left her feeling hollow. Which was good, because the alternative, to feel upset that he took what had happened last night for granted, would put her in an untenable position.

Suddenly Damen's lack of sensitivity felt like a blessing in disguise. If he didn't care then she didn't have to either.

'What do you want to know?'

He blinked and for a moment she could almost believe she'd discomfited him. Only for a moment.

'Everything. Who he is, what he is to you. What he did.'

Steph swallowed, her throat gritty. 'Not much, then.'

Yet had locking the past away like a shameful secret helped her deal with it? It wasn't as if she'd done anything wrong. Besides, with the money she was earning from Damen she had the power to undo the damage, financially if not personally. It would take a long time to trust again.

She swung away towards the bank of windows. Already the island was slipping away, the big yacht gathering speed as it headed for open water.

'His name's Jared and he was my boss. He managed a travel agency in Melbourne, though he didn't own it.'

'Just your boss?'

Steph frowned at the terse question but didn't bother turning. She kept her eyes on the creamy arc of sand that fringed the bay and the bright sparkle of sunlight on water. A couple of seabirds wheeled, pale against the brilliant blue sky.

'I looked on him as a mentor. Later he was my business partner.' She swallowed a bitter tang.

'You went into business together?'

Did he have to sound so surprised? 'I'm excellent at what I do. I brought in more business than anyone else in the team. Travel is my passion.' She paused, 'Well, other people's travel. I haven't done much myself.'

'You're a travel agent who hasn't travelled? I thought that was a perk of the job, trying out fabulous holiday destinations.'

Steph shrugged. 'I've travelled in Australia but not overseas. There was never time. I was always working.' Putting money aside for a secure future. 'Exploring the world was my dream. I almost went to South America but Gran got sick and...'

She stopped. He didn't need to know about Gran's cancer scare.

'So you became partners. In a new agency?'

Steph nodded. 'It was to specialise in bespoke, luxury travel. That's what I'm good at.' What she'd *been* good at. Who knew if she'd work in that field again?

Damen didn't say anything, just waited, and suddenly Steph wanted this over. 'We signed an agreement, pooled our resources, secured a loan and...' She stepped closer to the windows, putting out her hand to the wall of glass. 'He was going to put a deposit down on our new premises but instead he disappeared.'

'He had an accident?' Damen's voice came from just

over her shoulder and she turned to meet his stare. It was steady and unemotional.

'No accident. He simply took off. He cleared out the money we'd borrowed, the money I'd put up, even...' She stopped then shrugged. It was strangely cathartic telling the tale. Why not continue? 'I'd introduced him to my gran. What I didn't know was that he persuaded her to invest a chunk of her savings.' Steph dragged in a deep breath. 'The police are looking for him.'

Dark green eyes bored into her. 'That's why you wanted cash up front.'

He didn't sound happy. He sounded disapproving, as if she'd done something wrong, instead of being left high and dry by a fraudster.

Steph folded her arms again. 'It is. You have a problem with that?'

His brow furrowed. 'You should have told me.'

'Why? So you could lecture me on financial risk?' A flicker of familiar flame shot through her. 'I did everything right, everything by the book. How was I to know Jared would run when he got the cash?'

She shook her head. 'No, don't answer that. I'm sure you'd tell me I should have checked his background better, should have somehow divined he was a crook. Even though he had no criminal history.'

Steph swung away and stared at the fast-receding island. Would they return to Athens now? To days spent alone then evenings where Damen showed her off like a trophy? She shivered and rubbed her hands up her arms.

'Is there anything else? If not I'd like to go and lie down. It's been a...tiring couple of days.'

She felt him behind her, so close his warmth seeped into her. Even now, with her nerves jangling, she had a fantasy that he'd lean forward, put his arms around her and hold her close. Tell her he was sorry about what had happened with Jared. Tell her he was sorry they hadn't spent the day together because what he'd wanted, more than anything, was to be alone with her.

Because last night had been special.

She was special.

'Stephanie, I—'

'No!' Those couple of syllables didn't reveal any of the tenderness she'd come to crave last night. 'Not now. I need to rest.'

She spun on her heel and marched to the door. She'd had enough of men, and of Damen Nicolaides. She needed time alone.

CHAPTER TEN

DAMEN JABBED THE PUNCHBAG. Left, left, right. The quick blows should relieve the tension grabbing his shoulders and chest.

Not tonight. He'd been in the gym for forty minutes and was still wound too tight.

He turned away, unlacing the boxing gloves and scrubbing his face with a towel.

The problem was Stephanie and the nagging feeling he'd done the wrong thing.

He should have trusted his instincts. Not the familiar voice of caution that urged him to keep his distance, but the one that wanted to sweep her into his arms and his bed and keep her there.

He'd made a tactical error keeping his distance. It was clear she didn't want anything to do with him. He'd missed his chance for more intimacy. Strangely though, that wasn't the worst. The worst was knowing she was hurting and he was part of that hurt because he'd let her down.

Clio would say he felt this way because of his managing personality, because he'd shouldered responsibility for his family and the vast empire that was Nicolaides Shipping at a young age. Damen wasn't so sure. This felt different.

Stephanie wasn't family, yet he felt...

Damen shook his head. Better to stick to facts than feelings. Fact one. Last night had been phenomenal, and instead of thanking Stephanie, and looking after her when he guessed she was physically sore and possibly feeling out of her depth, he'd left her at first light then found excuses to keep away.

Fact two. She'd more than fulfilled her part of their bargain. Not only had she played her part in public but today she'd gone beyond what was necessary, helping Clio and her mother with this idea of a luxury retreat in Italy and even charming Manos. He hadn't seen his aunt look so relaxed in ages.

Fact three. Stephanie wasn't a gold-digger, eager for his money. She'd needed cash to make good money stolen from her and her grandmother.

Pain tore through Damen's belly as he imagined how she'd felt, discovering her business partner was a thief. That everything she'd worked towards was gone, and her grandmother's savings too.

Damen remembered his annoyance at having to pay for Stephanie's wardrobe in Athens and felt his skin crawl. He was so used to assuming people were avaricious he hadn't considered any other option.

That was one thing, at least, he'd rectified. He'd transferred the other million dollars into her account and discreet enquiries were being made in Melbourne to ensure that would cover the business loan she'd mentioned. Technically it wasn't Damen's debt and yet he felt he owed her.

He wasn't used to feeling guilty, as if he'd done the wrong thing. There must be something he could do to make it up to Stephanie.

Damen raked the towel around his neck then stopped, an idea forming.

She wanted to travel. It was her dream. He recalled all her outings in Athens to museums and ancient ruins, to markets and landmarks. She'd spent every moment of her free time exploring the city. No doubt she'd spend the next six weeks doing the same. Unless Damen changed his plans.

A smile eased across his face as he reached for the ship's phone.

Next morning Steph woke alone.

Of course she didn't miss Damen!

Yesterday she'd hoped for even a shadow of the intimacy they'd shared. Instead Damen had interrogated her about her past as if he was more interested in Jared than their lovemaking.

Even so, her thoughts were all of Damen.

Till she opened her curtains.

Steph stared, dumbfounded, at the view. She recognised it, of course, though the iconic vista, known the world over, was usually from above, looking down to where she was.

Beyond the window the sea was the rich blue of lapis lazuli. Rising from it were cliffs of deep ochre red and dark grey, frosted along the top with a canopy of white buildings, bright in the sun.

Santorini.

She breathed deep and blinked. From here she could make out a zigzag track up the slope that she knew was popular with tourists who paid to ride donkeys along the steep, cobblestoned road. She thought of the honeymoons she'd booked here for clients, the luxury hotels with terraces that seemed to hang out over the cliffs, the perfect venue for cocktails as the sun sank into the sea. The marvellous frescoes that had been discovered at the other end of the island, remnants of an ancient civilisation that had been shattered by a massive volcanic eruption. The fabled Atlantis, some said.

Steph almost danced with excitement as she dressed and hurried from her room.

Only to skid to a stop when she found Damen emerging from his stateroom at the same time.

'You look well,' he said. 'You had a good rest?'

It was crazy to feel a flicker of exultation at the sound of his voice. The man was just making polite conversation. Yet the impact of that deep tone and his penetrating forest-green stare was real.

'I did, thank you.'

He nodded but didn't move. His brows twitched together

and Steph had the curious idea that he hesitated, as if he wasn't sure how to proceed.

Damen Nicolaides, hesitating? Not possible. Yet, instead of turning away in search of breakfast, Steph waited, heart thudding high in her throat.

He reached a hand towards her then dropped it, the furrow deepening on his brow.

'I owe you an apology, for yesterday.'

Steph felt her eyebrows lift.

His gaze drifted away then slewed back, pinning her to the spot. 'I should have been there in the morning. When you woke. What we shared was...'

Steph held herself completely still, waiting.

'... Phenomenal. And I didn't even thank you.' Again his hand rose, this time to the back of his neck, as if the muscles there were tight.

They couldn't be as tight as Steph's. She didn't want a post mortem of that night, not if it entailed this stilted conversation. Two nights ago intimacy had seemed right, perfect. But now...

'I don't need your thanks.' She turned away, preferring not to meet that searching stare. 'You're not obligated to me.'

'Stephanie.' This time his voice was urgent. He stepped close, hemming her in. 'Please listen.'

Reluctantly she turned back. Damen met her gaze steadily. 'I'm trying, very badly, to apologise.' He spread his hands. 'What we shared was special. So special it threw me. Yesterday I didn't behave well. I should have checked you were okay and—'

'Of course I was okay. It was just sex.' Her voice was too strident, as if she tried to convince herself as well as him.

'Nevertheless, I apologise for deserting you. I went off to do some work but that's no excuse for poor behaviour.'

Stephanie wished the carpeted floor would open up and swallow her. Which was worse, Damen thinking she was so fragile she needed him by her side because she'd surrendered her virginity, as if she were some Victorian maiden? Or the decadent thrill of excitement stirring inside, hearing him admit what they'd shared was special?

Because that would mean she felt the same. That she wanted more of what she'd tasted that night in Damen's arms. The idea terrified her.

'Apology accepted.'

For a long moment Damen said nothing, his stare far too unsettling.

'Why are we at Santorini?' she said quickly. 'I thought we were returning to Athens.'

Damen drew her arm through his, leading her away from the staterooms. Steph tried not to react, though the feel of his arm on hers made her nerve endings jitter and heat pool low inside. 'I changed my mind. I can work from the *Amphitrite* a bit longer. You might as well see some of the islands while you're in Greece.'

Steph rocked to a halt. 'You came here for me?'

She frowned, trying to fathom what was going on. Damen didn't change his schedule for her. *She* fitted into his world.

'What do you want, Damen?' Carefully she slipped free of his hold. 'Why are you doing this?'

Because he wants more sex.

And that's good because you do too.

Ruthlessly Steph stifled the voice in her head. She had more self-respect than to give herself to him just because he'd arranged a treat. Even if it was a wonderful treat. Even if she wanted him as much now as she had two nights ago.

Damen tilted his head as if to get a clearer view of her face. 'You're helping me enormously, performing this charade, and you went further than you needed to yesterday, helping Clio and her mother. They really do need to get away and you've got them excited at the prospect.'

Steph shrugged. 'It wasn't difficult. It's what I do.'

'But you didn't *need* to. You did it because you're a nice person.'

Strange how those simple words resonated like the most lavish praise.

'I wanted to do something for you. You said you'd never had the chance to travel and here we are on the Aegean. It seemed selfish to sail back to Athens before you'd seen more of the islands.'

Dazed, Steph stared up into that handsome face. Every time she felt she understood Damen Nicolaides he pulled the rug out from under her feet.

'Come on.' He reached for her elbow and led her down the wide passage. 'The sooner we eat, the sooner you can explore.'

They stayed at Santorini for two days and to Steph's surprise Damen took several hours off from his work each day to accompany her ashore. Steph thought he'd be bored doing tourist things, seeing ancient frescoes, clambering up and down meandering streets and stopping every few metres as she found yet another spectacular view. But never once did he reveal impatience, though he admitted he preferred visiting when the crowds were thinner.

From Santorini they cruised east, calling at Astypalaia, Kos and Symi. Steph explored quaint towns, museums and ancient ruins, and swam in crystal waters. She'd never felt more relaxed and enthralled. Each day brought new discoveries, stunning vistas, friendly people and fascinating places.

It also brought hours with Damen, not at some exclusive party, but hand in hand as he led her through narrow streets, drank thick Greek coffee in the shade of vine-covered pergolas and told her about his country.

What surprised her most was that Damen seemed at home in such simple surroundings, far from the trappings of enormous wealth. And the fact that she enjoyed being with him. Enjoyed it too much to maintain a proud distance.

Back on the yacht they dined on deck, eating sumptuous meals perfectly prepared, and watching the sun set in a glow of tangerine over the dark sea. Each night, as they sat in the candlelight, it became harder for Steph to recall why she was angry with Damen.

Especially when she discovered he'd paid the second instalment of her contracted fee. Because, he said, he trusted her to make good on her contract and act the part of his lover for another six weeks. And because he didn't want her to suffer any more because of Jared's theft. He'd been concerned to learn about the joint loan they'd taken out and her ability to service the repayments.

It was amazing how wonderful it felt to have the burden of the lost money completely lifted from her shoulders.

His gesture rocked Steph. She'd thought Damen a man who'd stick to the letter of their agreement. She'd never expected such generosity, or trust.

No one in her life had shown such faith in her. With two exceptions: Gran and Emma. Steph understood how rare it was.

That action by Damen, extravagant and unexpected, confused her. It was too big a gesture. It evoked a raft of emotions she struggled to contain. Emotions she didn't know what to do with.

It would have been simpler if Damen had made a move on her, assuming that she'd agree to have sex again, partly because, as he said, it had been phenomenal, and partly out of gratitude.

Instead she was flummoxed to find he treated her like an honoured guest. He was charming and attentive but didn't press for intimacy. When they were ashore he played the part of lover in public with his arm around her waist, or feeding her delicacies from his plate, or whispering in her ear.

Steph got almost used to it. What she couldn't get used to was the way Damen's arm would drop from around her once they boarded his yacht and there was no need for a public display of affection.

What did that say about her?

It had been a week since they'd shared a bed. A week during which she'd gone to sleep each night recalling how magical that night had been. Her mind tortured her with steamy erotic dreams that left her wide awake in the early hours, heart pumping and body aching for fulfilment.

Damen had done that to her.

Except Steph knew that wasn't right.

She'd done it. She'd opened the Pandora's Box that was sexual desire. She'd chosen to seek physical release with Damen and now she bore the consequences. The fact that he was an amazing, generous lover only compounded the problem. If he'd been selfish in bed, a total disappointment, it would have made things so much easier.

Instead the memory of him, them, drove her crazy.

She wanted him. Badly. It was worse now she knew what she was missing. Especially spending this time with Damen, seeing the best of him, enjoying every day to the full. Even the casual brush of his arm against hers sent a thrill of wanting through her.

They emerged from deep shadow and walked out into the heat bouncing off the cobblestoned square. Automatically Steph turned around and stared back up at the thick, crenellated towers soaring up against the blue sky.

'My first visit to a castle.'

'I guessed.' Damen's voice was soft in her ear.

She turned to find those deep green eyes crinkling in amusement.

'There wasn't a centimetre of it you didn't examine. Especially the mosaics.'

He was right. She'd taken hundreds of photos. The Palace of the Grand Master of the Knights of Rhodes was a stunning building. It mightn't be filled to the brim with antiques but she'd strung out their visit, poring over every detail.

Steph's lips twitched. 'You're right and you've been so patient. I owe you. What would you like in return?'

Just like that the amusement faded from his eyes, banished by a hot glitter that sent fire curling through her blood. Steph's breath snagged and her heart pounded high and hard as if it tried to leap out of her chest.

Steph knew that look. She'd seen it the night they'd gone to bed together. And every night since in her lonely bed as she relived the thrill of being naked with Damen.

She licked dry lips, his gaze following the movement. The way he watched her was so…intimate, she felt it as if he reached out to trail his fingers across her mouth.

Abruptly he looked away, surveying the streets leading from the palace into the old town of Rhodes. It was a reminder that they were in public. She noticed some phones and cameras turned their way.

Had that look on Damen's face been for show?

She couldn't believe it. When they were out together Damen smiled at her but never once had she glimpsed that hot, hungry stare that turned her insides molten.

'I'm ready for a cool drink.' His hand closed around hers, sending a quiver of excitement through her. Steph curled her fingers into his and let him lead her, not down the main street but into a picturesque alley that was blessedly cool, with high stone buildings on either side. Beaten copper pots hung outside an artisan's workshop, gleaming even in the shadows.

Damen led her down the lane, taking a side turning and then another, till they were in a street so narrow Steph could almost touch the walls on each side. Then on their left was an open door, a small, shaded courtyard with rush-bottomed chairs and tiny tables.

Minutes later she was sipping gratefully from an iced glass. But the cold drink didn't quench the heat that had erupted at Damen's blatantly possessive stare outside the palace.

It was a warm day, even in the trellised shade, even with the icy drink. But not that hot. The fiery heat came from within. She put her glass down and turned to Damen. Predictably he was already regarding her, his gaze steady but unreadable.

'What's wrong? You're not enjoying yourself now.'

The man was too perceptive. He saw things she preferred he didn't.

No, that wasn't right. Steph couldn't lie to herself any longer. She liked it when they were both on the same page. When it took just a look and they were in agreement. It happened increasingly as they spent time together and she discovered Damen was far more than a bossy tycoon. He was a man with a sense of humour, with patience and much more.

'It's not that. Visiting Rhodes is the best. I've wanted to come here for so long. And it's every bit as wonderful as I thought.'

'But?'

Steph's pulse thudded as she held his eyes.

She could prevaricate.

Or she could trust her instinct.

'Perhaps there's something else you'd like even more than exploring a medieval city.' He paused, his eyes glittering like shards of precious gems. 'I know there's something else *I* want.'

'What do you want, Damen?'

He leaned close. 'To kiss you on the lips. To take you in my arms. To make love to you.'

Steph's breath escaped in a sigh that felt like relief. 'I want that too.'

The words were barely out when he stood, drawing her up beside him, tossing some money onto the table.

His mouth curved into a smile that threatened to unstring her knees. 'Then what are we waiting for, *agapi mou*?'

* * *

If he'd cared about such things Damen would have been annoyed at his total lack of cool as he strode through the wind-
ing streets of old Rhodes, back to the harbour. A couple of
times Stephanie almost had to trot to keep up, but she didn't
complain. Far from it. Her eyes glowed in anticipation, and
whenever he glanced at her beside him it was all he could
do not to scoop her up in his arms and break into a run.

She was so deliciously alluring. Damen couldn't believe
how lucky he was.

They made it back onto the yacht in a breathless rush that
made him feel like a reckless teenager. Except that wasn't
quite right. Oh, the rampant lust was there, but beneath it
was something else. Caring, admiration, something deeper
than he'd felt in his youthful testosterone-fuelled amours.

Damen didn't release her hand as they marched through
the yacht to his stateroom. The door swung shut and he
turned to face Stephanie.

Her breasts rose rapidly as if, like he, she had trouble
capturing enough air. Her eyes were wide with a saucy excitement that drilled heat straight to his loins.

'You wanted to kiss me.'

'Yes.' His voice emerged as a rasp.

'I wish you'd hurry up. It's been so long.'

Beneath her bodice Stephanie's nipples peaked in invitation. His body tightened.

'I want more than that.' Why he held back he didn't fully
understand. To be sure she needed this as much as he did?
He couldn't be the only one to feel this desperation. 'I want
everything. Once I touch you...' He spread his hands.

Stephanie smiled. A sultry smile that lifted the corners
of her mouth and shimmered in her gold-toned eyes. It was
bewitching. So must Circe have smiled on Odysseus, lur-
ing him. It was hard to believe that a week ago Stephanie
had been a virgin.

Damen's hands cupped her cheeks as he took her mouth, plundering deep into her sweetness, sealing her lips with his.

It was everything he remembered and more. He was only dimly aware of their surroundings as he backed her across the room till her legs touched the bed and he tumbled them both onto it.

Stephanie was all satiny limbs, ardent mouth and soft, eager body. Her fingers ripped at his shirt as he shoved her skirt up.

The next moments were a blur of building excitement. His shirt came off, and then his belt. Stephanie's lacy underwear came away in his hand with one forceful tug. The sound of it ripping fed a frenzy for completion that he only just managed to leash.

'Condom,' he gasped, forcing himself to move away.

Stephanie's hands were busy with his trousers as he reached for the bedside table, tearing a packet open with his teeth. Seconds later, sheathed, he settled between her bare legs, her skirt rucked up beneath his bare torso, her eyes heavy-lidded in anticipation.

She was glorious.

Damen made himself pause, hefted a breath that felt like agony as his lungs heaved.

A hand between her legs confirmed she was ready. He palmed her thigh, smooth and supple, and lifted it high. She lifted the other one too, hooking it over his bare hip, and something dived deep in his belly. It was a swooping sensation that heralded the end of his control.

Damen lowered his head and took her mouth again, glorying in the way she opened for him, like a flower to sunshine. He tilted his hips, finding the spot he needed and moving slowly, inexorably, alert to any sign of discomfort. Stephanie gasped against his mouth, lifted her pelvis and wrapped her legs tight around his hips, locking him to her.

He had a moment to glory in the perfection that was

their joining. But only a moment. For he needed to move, withdraw and glide back again, harder this time and faster.

Stephanie's breath expelled in a soft *oof* of air against his lips as her hands clawed his bare shoulders.

Another thrust, this time met by a perfectly timed lift of her hips that sent flickering sensation from his groin to his spine and up to the back of his skull where his skin pulled tight. Everything pulled tight.

'Stephanie,' he growled, turned on even by the sound of her name on his tongue.

Her palms lifted to his cheeks as she put her mouth to his and bit his lower lip.

Liquid heat seared him, incinerating control.

He gathered her close, angling till he felt Stephanie's giveaway judder of response, then thrusting home again and again until she broke apart in his arms and he fell with her into the vast, consuming wave of ecstasy.

Damen held her tight, thoughts disintegrating under that powerful onslaught.

As he slowly came back to himself, Damen had enough sense to roll onto his back so as not to crush her. He took Stephanie with him, cradling her.

It took a long time for his brain to crank into gear. When it did he was torn between satisfaction and consternation.

Because he was certain of one thing. He wanted more than six weeks with Stephanie. Their allotted time wouldn't be nearly enough to make the most of this explosive attraction.

Inevitably his mind went to Ingrid, who'd seduced his younger self with sex and a display of affection that had been as false as her promises.

Ingrid, who'd made him dance to her tune, all the way, almost, to the altar.

As ever, his thoughts slewed away from that. There'd be no altar, no marriage in Damen's future. That was the one thing of which he was absolutely sure. The very thought made him break into a cold sweat. Because tangled with that thought was the memory of the tragedy he'd created, which affected his family to this day.

Damen wasn't certain what this connection to Stephanie meant for his well-ordered life, but he wasn't stupid enough to ignore something so profound. So pleasurable.

His lips curved in a lazy smile as he smoothed his hand over her damp, flushed skin and she arched beneath his touch, her sated body responsive even now.

So it was settled. He'd keep Stephanie with him beyond the term of their contract. He'd talk to her about it later. As soon as he worked out the terms of a new arrangement that would satisfy them both.

CHAPTER ELEVEN

STEPHANIE'S PULSE THROBBED so fast and hard she put a hand out to the door jamb, steadying herself. She was light-headed, but only, she assured herself, because she was nervous. More nervous than she'd ever been in her life.

One slow breath. Another.

They didn't help much.

Nothing would help, till she could dismiss the suspicion that had gnawed at her the last few days.

She'd left Rhodes in a rosy haze of delight. Stephanie had barely been aware of their surroundings, so wrapped up was she in Damen. Even his apology about returning to Athens for necessary meetings hadn't punctured her happiness.

They took several days sailing to the capital and spent most of the time together. When Damen worked, Steph caught up on her sleep. Which was just as well, since Damen usually woke her with the devil in his eyes and seduction in those clever hands.

Increasingly Steph wondered where this relationship might lead. For, great as the sex was, it *was* a relationship. That, more than anything, was what had taken her unawares. Sexual compatibility she'd been prepared for, but this…this was more.

They talked, sharing information about themselves, often small things, it was true, but it felt as if she was finally coming to understand this complex man and he her. He even told her about his sisters, clearly proud of their achievements. They laughed and found pleasure in each other's company, even when they were too exhausted to make love. Or when she was. Damen had a stamina that astounded her, but he tempered it with concern for her wellbeing, as if she were still an untried innocent.

Innocent! Her mouth tightened as she surveyed the sitting room of his penthouse. It was designer-elegant with sculptures and other artworks that could have graced a museum. The morning view over Athens was stupendous and even the floral arrangements cost more than she'd spend in a week on food in Melbourne.

What she and Damen shared felt wonderful, so wonderful she didn't want to question too closely where it might lead. As if by doing so she'd tempt fate to end it. Yet in the cold, hard light of day some might look at this arrangement and say he'd bought her company.

Steph's stomach clenched and nausea stirred.

No! That wasn't what this was.

This relationship was about mutual attraction and respect. Despite the money he'd paid her for the charade, in their *real* relationship they were equals. Each giving freely of themselves. Neither expecting nor demanding anything long term.

Long term...

Another unsettling swirl of nausea.

Steph straightened. It was time to scotch the anxiety that had been nibbling away at her since she realised her period was late.

She looked at the pregnancy kit she'd bought from the chemist down the road as soon as it opened. It was just a precaution. The chances of pregnancy were ninety-nine point something per cent against, since Damen had used a condom every time.

Of course it would be a false alarm.

'I gather congratulations are in order.' Christo's voice on the end of the line didn't sound congratulatory. It sounded terse.

'Sorry?' Damen turned his back on the now empty conference table and strode to the windows looking out on the sea, darkening as the sun set. The headquarters of Nicolaides Shipping faced the harbour of Piraeus, a reminder of the company's focus and the source of its vast wealth. 'Are you back from your honeymoon already?'

'No. But Emma will be concerned when she reads the reports so I thought I'd get the story from you first.'

Damen frowned. 'You've lost me. What story?'

'You don't know?'

'Christo, I don't have time for guessing games. I've got my hands full with major negotiations.'

He rolled his shoulders. That last meeting had been long and trying, but his plans to re-establish his firm's shipbuilding capacity in Greece might finally come to fruition. In his father's day all that had moved offshore to places where costs were cheaper. Damen was determined that at least some of that work would return to his own country, his contribution to the local economy.

'You and Stephanie. You're in the press.'

'Is that all?' Damen smiled as he thought of Stephanie. Persuading her to be his companion was surely his most brilliant idea.

Manos had backed off. Clio was ecstatic. But most important of all was Stephanie herself. He couldn't recall the last time a woman had made him feel so good. So full of anticipation just at the thought of seeing her at the end of the day.

He'd known she was special from the start. The attraction between them was explosive and showed no signs of diminishing. He liked spending time with her out of bed too. She was bright and fun and genuine and he wanted her to stay in Greece past the end of their contract. He wasn't foolish enough to expect what they had to last. Damen knew not to expect permanency. But for the foreseeable future…

'All? You don't sound fazed.'

'Of course not.' He made himself focus on Christo. 'Stephanie…' He paused. He preferred not to mention the money she'd accepted from him. Christo might get the wrong idea about her. 'She agreed to stay with me for a couple of months. To play the part of my girlfriend. I was getting heat from another quarter to marry and you know that's impossible.'

'Is it?'

Damen frowned. Christo was one of the few who knew the details of his past. Though even he didn't know it all. 'Of course. You know I'll never marry.'

Christo muttered something that sounded like a curse. 'You're saying the latest reports aren't true? I can tell Emma the gossip online is wrong?'

Damen hesitated. Their relationship might have begun as a charade but it was more now. Damen planned to ask Stephanie to stay with him, past the expiry of their agreement, until their passion died a natural death. Something that burned so brightly must destroy itself eventually. But there was no reason they shouldn't make the most of it while it lasted.

'Stephanie and I…enjoy each other's company.'

'And?'

'Isn't that enough?' No doubt gossip was ramping up because Damen didn't have live-in lovers. He valued his privacy too much and didn't trust women not to get the idea they could worm their way into his life permanently. But Stephanie was different.

'So you're sharing a bed. All the world knows that, except Emma, so far. She'll get her hopes up about the pair of you when she finds out. But this new rumour…'

'What new rumour?' Damen frowned. Why were they wasting time discussing paparazzi gossip?

'You really don't know?' There was a strange note in his friend's voice. 'Then it's unfounded gossip. I knew you'd never—'

'Never what?' Damen spoke through gritted teeth.

There was a pause, long enough to hear his pulse beat once, twice, three times.

'Get her pregnant. A story broke today that you're expecting a child together.'

Shock jabbed Damen, before reason took over. He laughed, assuring his friend that the gossip-mongers were inventing a story where there was none.

His good humour lasted until, trawling through so-called news reports, he saw a photo of Stephanie on the street outside his apartment, smiling directly into the camera. Below it, the article said:

An excited Stephanie Logan, Damen Nicolaides' girlfriend, confided it was early days, with the pregnancy only a few weeks along.

Stephanie felt trapped. She didn't want to go out after what had happened on the street this morning, when a man had shoved a camera in her face. But nor did she feel like asking if Damen's driver could take her sightseeing.

Not when her world had just turned upside down.

Pregnant. She was pregnant with Damen's child.

Even now, hours after seeing the pregnancy test results, she couldn't process it.

How could she be pregnant? Yet she'd heard stories about people who'd conceived despite protection.

Her hand crept to her abdomen. Was it true? Was a new life forming there? She told herself she wouldn't be certain till she'd had the test confirmed by a doctor, yet she *felt* different. When she crossed her arms her breasts were sensitive. That, combined with her late period, had sent her scurrying to the chemist.

It had been embarrassing, explaining to a stranger what she wanted, but she'd needed help to find the kit and translate the instructions.

Maybe she'd done it wrong? Maybe it was a false positive?

She was clutching at straws.

Steph planted her hands on the railing of the penthouse terrace and tried to still her whirling thoughts. She had no plan for the future. All she felt was shock.

And a tiny seed of what might be excitement.

Because, no matter how unexpected, there was something thrilling as well as terrifying about the prospect of a baby.

She narrowed her eyes against the glare of late sun on the pale city.

All her life she'd told herself she wouldn't make her mother's mistakes. She'd be independent financially and emotionally. No struggling as a single mum to make ends meet. It was true that, thanks to Damen's money, she was able to repay the money she owed, and her gran's money, and have some left for herself.

But she'd still be a single mother.

An unemployed single mother. Despite the cushion of cash in her account, she'd have to find a job eventually.

Steph dragged in a deep breath, filled with fear.

It wasn't simply fear about the burdens of bringing up a child. Selfishly it was as much about herself and Damen. About what this news meant for them. She hadn't let herself hope for permanency with him. But the prospect of losing him now made her feel hollow with pain.

This news would end their idyll.

She wrapped her arms around herself. Was it selfish to worry about that when she should be worrying about the new life inside her?

The undeniable truth was that Damen *mattered* to her, far more than she'd let herself believe. *They* mattered as a couple. What they had was so fragile, so new, yet it felt profound. Not like a fling at all.

For her.

But for him?

'Enjoying the sunset?' Damen's voice reached out from

the shadows, curling like a lasso around her middle and drawing tight.

Steph swung round, a relieved smile tugging at her lips. Despite her nerves, despite everything, she felt better now Damen was here.

What did that say about how far she'd come from the fiercely independent, fiercely distrustful woman who'd arrived in Greece last month?

Steph feared it said everything.

The way she felt about Damen—

'Nothing to say, Stephanie?' He stepped further onto the terrace, the sunset burnishing his face to stark bronze. He looked like an ancient warrior, proud and relentless. A shiver scuttled down her spine.

This wasn't the lover she'd known the last few weeks.

It wasn't even the managing billionaire who'd expected her to fall in with his outrageous plans.

Steph looked into blazing eyes that nevertheless made her bones frost. This was a stranger. A man she didn't know. Something almost like fear stirred at the base of her spine.

'Damen. I didn't expect you yet.' He'd mentioned late meetings.

'I found I couldn't keep away.' His lips curled at the corners, but instead of forming a smile his expression looked more like a grimace.

'What's wrong? Has something happened?' She walked towards him, thinking of his mother, of Clio and the others she'd met at the wedding. Or maybe he'd had bad news about one of his sisters.

'I thought you could tell me.' He paused, his brow drawing down in the middle. 'Have you got news for me?'

'How did you know?' She goggled up at him, stunned.

'Call it a hunch.'

Steph frowned. She'd told nobody. Even without the time difference from Greece, she couldn't talk to Gran about this yet, or Emma, who was still on her honeymoon. First she had to come to grips with the news. And talk to Damen. She hadn't looked at her phone all day, worried that if she started searching for information on pregnancy she'd scare herself silly.

'A hunch?' She shook her head. 'How—?'

'What's your news, Stephanie?'

Dubiously she stared at him. Every sense told her something was wrong. He couldn't know about the baby. Yet...

'You might want to sit down.'

Instead he simply folded his arms over his chest. His body language worried her. She told herself she was upset, misreading his non-verbal cues.

'Okay, then.' She drew a slow breath. 'I took a pregnancy test this morning. And it appears I'm pregnant.'

Nothing. Not a word for two whole beats of her heart.

'Appears?'

Steph frowned. He didn't look surprised.

'I *am* pregnant.' Now it came to the crunch she was sure of it. 'Though I'd like to check with a doctor.'

'How very convenient.'

She blinked and it was as if the movement dragged the scales from her eyes. For now she read Damen's expression. Anger laced with disdain.

At *her*!

Her head reared back. 'It's not my fault. You can't think I engineered this. There were two of us having sex.'

Making love, that was how it had felt, but she couldn't say that, not when he looked at her with fury in those glittering eyes.

A chill iced her to the marrow. Steph stepped back till she came up against the railing. Horrified, she told herself not to cringe. She'd done nothing wrong!

'You were the one to handle protection.'

If anything the reminder only stoked his anger. His eyes narrowed and his jaw tightened. It was a wonder steam didn't come out of his ears.

'You really think I'm so gullible?' His words were soft but tinged with menace.

Sternly Steph reminded herself Damen might be furious but he wasn't dangerous.

'You might not want to believe it, Damen, but it's true.' She stared up at him, refusing to be cowed by that pulsing anger. 'You might not like the surprise but I'd thought you a better man than to react like this.'

His hand sliced the air dismissively. 'Stop now. I know this is a con.'

'Sorry?' She'd expected surprise, but nothing like this.

'I know you've contrived this. You should stop while you're ahead.'

Abruptly, gloriously, it was Steph seeing red. Contrived, indeed! Did he think she'd engineered a lie to—what? Trap him into a long-term relationship?

Steph gasped as the pieces clicked into place and she realised that was exactly what he thought. The monstrous ego of the man!

It didn't matter that mere minutes ago she'd realised she…cared for him much more than she should. That the idea of ending their affair tore at her heart. She'd like to slap him for his egotistical arrogance.

Steph swung away and marched inside.

'Don't walk away from me! We haven't finished.'

Too bad. Steph refused to stand there, an unwilling target for his poisonous barbs.

She strode to the bathroom off the master bedroom, swiping the test result off the marble counter. When she turned it was to find Damen filling the doorway. He was a tall man, broad-shouldered and well-built, but anger seemed to make him even bigger. Steph didn't care. She crossed the space and shoved the plastic into his hand.

'What's this?' But his eyes were rounding as he spoke. His olive-gold skin paled a couple of shades.

'Proof.' Steph folded her arms tight across her heaving chest. 'I went to the chemist and bought a kit.'

But Damen was already shaking his head. 'Of course you've somehow got hold of a positive result. The bluff wouldn't work otherwise.'

'Bluff? I don't understand.'

His steely gaze captured hers. 'You really are a good actress, Stephanie. First class. But I know this is a lie. Otherwise why leak the news to the press? You're trying to force my hand.'

She shook her head. 'You're not making sense.' Had he had an accident? A blow to the head? But no, he looked pulsing with vibrant energy.

For answer he pulled a phone from his pocket, thumbed the screen and held it out to her.

Shock Baby Revelation for Nicolaides CEO!

That was as far as Steph got, as the words began to run together. But that was enough. That and the photo of her taken this morning.

A trembling began in her knees, turning into racking shudders. Her stomach, empty because she'd been too agitated to eat lunch, lurched. The room swayed, or maybe it was her.

Big hands grabbed her arms, half hauling, half lifting her across the room and onto the deeply cushioned seat beside the sunken bath. Damen forced her head down between her knees and slowly the awful sick feeling receded.

'Let me go.' She shook him off. 'I'm not going to be sick.'

Yet horror lingered at the back of her mouth. Steph took her time, breathing slowly, confronting the fact that her precious secret had become fodder for a sleazy press story. Eventually she realised that must be why Damen had come back looking like some merciless god seeking vengeance.

But how...?

'How did they get the story if you didn't tell them? Why did you smile for that photo if you weren't colluding with them?' His voice was hard but she saw something like concern in his assessing eyes, as if the sight of her weak and upset bothered him.

'I didn't. I smiled at the doorman to your building. He's always so friendly and today he helped me, directing me to a chemist. But as I came back to the apartment some guy with a big camera got in my way just as I was saying hi.'

She lifted the phone still clutched in her hand. Yes. It made sense. That was when the photo had been taken. By the man in the T-shirt of bilious green.

Steph frowned. 'It was him!'

'What is it? What did he do?'

Damen hunkered before her. He didn't touch her but he was so close his body heat blanketed her. She shivered, suddenly aware of how cold she felt.

'Stephanie?'

Muzzily she looked up into those brilliant eyes. If she didn't know better she'd say he looked worried. Except that would mean Damen cared when instead he thought she'd constructed a hoax and sold her story to the press.

'You think I went to the media with a story that I was pregnant? Why? For the cash they'd give for a scoop? Or to force your hand into a long-term commitment? Because you wouldn't kick me out if I was pregnant?'

Her voice was a shallow rasp but he heard her and his expression told her everything she needed to know.

Wearily she held out the phone to him then leaned back in the chair, closing her eyes. She didn't want to deal with the media stories or Damen.

'Tell me about the man, Stephanie.' His voice was soft, persuasive yet still compelling.

She wanted to yell at him, demand he leave her alone, that he go and take his massive ego with him. But she didn't have the energy. All day she'd been wound so tight and now she felt totally undone.

'Stephanie, talk to me.'

He palmed her cheek with a warm hand just as he'd done when they made love. It sent pain arrowing through her, a jab to the heart. She wrenched her head away, snapping her eyes open to glare at him.

'Don't. Touch. Me.'

Something ripped across Damen's expression, something she couldn't name and didn't want to.

'Please, Stephanie. Tell me about the man.'

She sighed. She was tempted to let him work it out himself but what was the point?

'The man with the camera, who took the photo. He wore a distinctive green T-shirt. He was there in the chemist when I was.'

'Did you talk to him?'

'No. I just spoke to the pharmacist. I needed help finding a pregnancy kit and getting instructions on how to use it.' She paused, frowning. The other guy had browsed for something in the next aisle.

'Did you tell the pharmacist anything else?'

'I didn't give him my name or yours, if that's what you're thinking.' She paused. 'I did ask if it would work in the very early stages of pregnancy because I couldn't be more than a few weeks along.'

Damen's expression changed, hard lines marking his features.

'What?'

'That's what they wrote in the press, that the...pregnancy was in the early stages.'

'So maybe they got that from the pharmacist or the man with the camera.' She sat straighter. 'They certainly didn't get it from me. I was hoping it was a false alarm, that I wasn't really pregnant.' Her voice dipped on the word as the enormity of the situation hit her. 'If I was going to tell someone it wouldn't be the press, no matter what you think.'

'I believe you.'

'Sorry?'

Sombre eyes met hers. Damen held his phone out to her. 'Is this the man you saw?'

She peered at a grainy photo. 'Different clothes but that's him.'

'He's paparazzi. He's been hanging around since we got back to Athens. Security moved him on but not effectively enough. He probably followed you from the apartment building.' Damen drew a slow breath. 'I owe you an apology.'

'You do.'

'I'm sorry, Stephanie. I shouldn't have doubted you. I should have known better.'

'You should.' It had hurt terribly that he'd jumped to such a vile conclusion about her. 'I thought we were beginning to know each other.' That had been the worst part. That he knew her now, or should, yet still he'd thought the worst.

Damen's mouth flattened, but then he nodded. 'You're right.' He drew a deep breath. 'I've spent a long time learning to be suspicious, especially of women. It's a hard habit to break. I can't tell you how sorry I am.'

Steph wanted to know why he was suspicious of women. But this wasn't the time to pursue it. She felt appallingly light-headed. Shock, she supposed.

It was as if he read her mind. 'Would you feel better lying down?'

She nodded but before she could stand Damen slid his arms around her and lifted her high against his chest. Steph didn't need to be carried. But her legs felt like overcooked pasta and, despite everything, it was comforting to rest her head against his shoulder. She didn't even protest when he took her to the master suite. She'd fight that out with him later, when she had more energy.

Damen laid her on the bed and took her shoes off, pulling a light blanket over her. It was like when she was a child and Gran had taken care of her when she got ill. Except she wasn't a child and Damen was nothing like Gran.

Then he confounded her by pressing a kiss to her brow.

'Rest now. The doctor will be here soon.'

'Doctor?' She scrambled up onto one elbow.

'You said you'd like to see a doctor. I'll feel better too. You're as white as a sheet.'

Steph lay back and watched him march out of the room. He meant it. There was concern on that wide brow and in his clenched jaw.

For her wellbeing?

Or because he needed to know for sure if she was pregnant?

To her dismay Steph discovered she wanted it to be for her. Because that would mean Damen cared.

It was dangerous, wishful thinking, the sort that could get her into trouble.

Except she was already in as deep as it went. For though she smarted at Damen's suspicions and wasn't in a forgiving mood, she'd realised something today that changed everything.

She'd fallen in love with Damen Nicolaides.

CHAPTER TWELVE

DAMEN STARED INTO the darkness. It was well past midnight and he needed sleep. Tomorrow there'd be vital negotiations and decisions. Yet sleep eluded him.

His brain raced, sifting the day's events. Confirmation from the doctor that Stephanie was pregnant, and, despite his fears at seeing her so weak, essentially well. And the unholy mess he'd made of things, shattering the trust he'd built with Stephanie.

Distrust came naturally to a man who'd been pursued all his life by those wanting a piece of his wealth. It became his default mode after Ingrid and her scheme to marry him, not for love, as she'd made him believe, but for money. The fact that fiasco—his fault for being gullible—had resulted in his father's death...

Damen's chest cramped as memories rose. But he didn't allow them to tug him into that black vortex of regret. He couldn't afford to, not with Stephanie's news. He needed to focus on the future.

His arms tightened around her, soft and trusting in his embrace. She was burrowed against him, head under his chin, her arm around his waist. It was all he could do not to wake her and lose himself in her sweet, welcoming body.

That moment this evening when she'd shied from his touch as if it were poisoned, when she'd looked at him with hurt branded in that shimmering stare...

That had pierced him to the core.

He deserved her disdain. Yet he hadn't been able to keep away. There'd be hell to pay tomorrow when she realised they'd shared a bed.

She'd been asleep when he'd entered, curled in a ball as if to protect herself from forces beyond her control. Damen had tasted guilt, like chilled metal on his tongue, knowing he was responsible for her distress.

He'd come to check on her, concerned despite the doctor's reassurances. But he'd been unable to walk away when she looked so vulnerable.

It had felt natural to strip off and get into bed, purely so he could be sure she was okay in the night. When she'd turned to him in her sleep…as she had every other night recently…of course he'd cuddled her, doing his best to assuage the hurt he'd caused.

But their closeness brought no relief.

Instead it magnified the size of their problem.

He grimaced. How skewed were his priorities to see a child as a problem?

It wasn't that he didn't like kids. It was that, after Ingrid and his fatal error in judgement, he'd known he'd never have children.

Now he would. He tried to imagine a child with his nose or the trademark Nicolaides stubbornness. Instead he saw a little girl with curls and golden-brown eyes. Stephanie holding her.

His breath snagged. Excitement stirred. A thrill of delight. And possessiveness.

He knew without a moment's doubt that he wanted this baby. Would do everything to care for and protect it.

Did Stephanie even want the child? The thought of her terminating the pregnancy made him break into a cold sweat.

Surely that wasn't likely. He couldn't imagine Stephanie taking that step.

What, then? The child was his too. He wanted to be part of its life. No. More. He wanted to be a full-time father. His family was close-knit and family ties were an ingrained part of him.

Damen had to persuade Stephanie to stay in Greece and

raise the child together. Or, if that wouldn't work, let him raise it without her.

His mind darted from one possibility to another. He could offer her money to relinquish the baby.

Right. As if that would work.

Stephanie had taken his money once but only because of her financial distress. Offering money now would set her against him. She wasn't avaricious. She was grounded, honest, honourable. She'd make a great mother.

He doubted she could be bought.

Did he even want to try?

Pain rayed through his jaw from grinding his teeth.

He needed Stephanie here, with him. Their baby deserved to have both parents.

But there was nothing to bind Stephanie here, to guarantee he'd have his child permanently.

Another contract? Without the lure of money, what could he offer to persuade her to stay?

What would cement his role as a full-time father?

He refused to consider being in his child's life for half of each year or just for holidays.

Could he appeal to Stephanie's maternal instincts? Persuade her two parents were better than one?

Stephanie shifted and Damen relaxed his hold, all the time searching for something that would bind her and their child to him.

There had to be something. If not money, then...

He grimaced as he tasted a familiar sour tang.

There was one way to secure a permanent role in his child's life.

The one thing he'd vowed on his father's grave to avoid.

Marriage.

Damen's breath whistled from his lungs and his heart set up a rough, catapulting rhythm. Nausea churned and his skin prickled as a decade of self-disgust and regret scoured him.

He couldn't do it.

There had to be another way. He had all night to find an alternative. Anything but that.

'Ochi, Baba. Ochi!'

This time Steph caught Damen's husky words. Before they'd been just a hoarse mumble of Greek. His head turned and he flung an arm across the bed.

She'd woken as the mattress moved beneath her, only to discover it wasn't the mattress but Damen. She'd been lying across him, cosily curled up in his big bed.

The room was dark and she blearily wondered how they had come to be sharing when she realised Damen was in the throes of a nightmare. He was scorching hot, as if with fever, his legs shifting restlessly as if trying to run.

She sat up and he instantly rolled away, clawing the bedding, his voice urgent, shoulders heaving.

Steph knew distress. This was real, and, despite her earlier anger, seeing him like this made her heart turn over.

Damen was controlled and strong. Even in anger he was composed. Only when they made love—

No, she wasn't going there.

'Damen.' She grabbed his shoulder, slippery with damp heat. 'Wake up.'

He turned, flinging out an arm that caught her on the elbow. He mumbled, and in the gloom she saw his ferocious scowl.

'Wake up. You're having a nightmare.' She put her other hand on his cheek, feeling bristles scratch her palm. It reminded her of the nights they'd slept together after hours of…no, not lovemaking, but sex.

She knew this man intimately, or so she'd thought. Till he'd stalked in tonight like an avenging angel.

Yet his fury hadn't lasted, had it? Only a few minutes into their argument and he'd been hunkering down before her, concerned and gentle.

Steph shook him harder. She refused to make excuses for appalling behaviour. How dared he accuse her of selling stories to the press?

Except she remembered goggling at Clio as she recounted the lengths women had gone to to snare Damen Nicolaides. Bribing hotel staff so they could wait, naked, in his bed. The short-lived paternity suit by a woman who, it was soon proved, had never even met him.

She leaned closer. 'Quick, Damen. You need to wake up!'

His eyes started open. For a long moment he stared blindly up at her. Then his hands curled around her shoulders.

'Stephanie? What is it? Are you all right?'

He sat up in a rush, his gaze darting around the room as if searching for a threat, then coming to rest on her. Those strong hands stroked down her arms.

'What is it? Are you ill? What can I do?'

And just like that, Steph's righteous indignation faded. He'd done wrong but he did care. Really care.

'Stephanie, tell me!' His urgency tugged at her heartstrings. Ridiculously she found herself blinking tears.

'I'm okay. It's you. You were having a nightmare.'

His grip tightened around her wrists. His chest rose on an audible, uneven breath.

'A nightmare.'

'You were thrashing around. It must have been a bad one.'

'Was I?' His voice sounded flat. He dropped his hands and she felt suddenly bereft. 'I apologise. I didn't mean to wake you. You need rest.'

This wasn't about her. He'd been so tortured. 'Do you have nightmares often?'

'Never.' He dragged a hand across his scalp in a gesture she knew signalled he wasn't as in control as he wanted her to believe.

'And this time?'

Damen's voice hadn't merely been agitated. He'd sounded as if his heart were being torn out.

'I don't recall.' He turned and retrieved the pillow that he'd pushed off the bed, leaving her staring at bare shoulders and the streamlined curve of his spine.

So very strong and yet, it seemed, vulnerable.

Curiosity rose. What did he dream that distressed him so? Something to do with their baby?

'I apologise for waking you, Stephanie. Shall we try to sleep?'

He had the decency at least not to lie down and assume she'd spend the rest of the night with him. He sat, hair tousled, big frame tense, watching her.

She should move to another room. Or demand he go.

She had a right to privacy.

Except she craved the comfort of Damen cradling her as much as ever.

She wanted to bridge the gulf between them, not widen it.

Silently she nodded and lay down. Damen drew a light cover over them both and sank onto the pillow beside her.

'I promise not to disturb you again.'

How could he promise that? The only way to prevent another nightmare was to stay awake all night.

She opened her mouth to ask him about it, then stopped. He wouldn't answer her questions. He'd made that clear.

But he had revealed something. She knew very little Greek but she knew *ne* was yes and *ochi* was no. She'd also heard Clio's sister calling her father *Baba*, which Steph assumed meant Dad.

Damen had been dreaming of his father, shouting, 'No, Dad, no!'

Something about his father stressed him unbearably. Something one of them had done or not done?

Was the nightmare triggered by today's news?

Steph wrapped her arms around her middle and rolled away to stare, wide-eyed, into the dark.

* * *

'I keep telling you, I'm perfectly fine. Yesterday was an aberration.' Steph saw a pulse tick at Damen's jaw but eventually he nodded.

Damen's concern was pleasant but she didn't need cosseting, or being told to rest when what she wanted was exercise. A walk or maybe a swim. After yesterday's fiasco with the paparazzi she'd content herself with a swim in the rooftop pool.

'Aren't you going to work?' They'd slept late and now lingered over breakfast on the terrace. Usually Damen had left for the office by now.

'Not today. We need to talk.'

Looking into that handsome face, tight with tension, Steph felt her stomach dip.

'I'm having the baby,' she blurted. She'd spent yesterday examining every option and knew that was non-negotiable.

'Good.' His mouth eased into a smile. 'I'm glad.'

'You are?'

Crazy that her heart thumped at his approval, or maybe just at the sight of his smile. Surely loving someone didn't make you so completely vulnerable to them? Steph was still her own woman. That wouldn't alter.

'Absolutely. Family is important. Of course I want this child.'

His starkly possessive tone simultaneously thrilled her and made her skin prickle with apprehension.

'*Our* child.' This baby wasn't his alone.

'Exactly. Our child, our responsibility.' He nodded and offered her more fresh orange juice. 'It's early, I know,' he said, 'but have you thought about the future?'

'Of course.' She'd peppered the doctor with questions about pregnancy, about diet and vitamins. Beyond that loomed the scary prospect of childbirth and motherhood. Steph didn't have much experience with babies. She had a lot to learn.

'So have I.' He paused. 'I have a proposition.'

Steph looked up from her bowl of yoghurt drizzled with honey and nuts to find him watching her closely. His smile had gone and he looked as serious as she'd ever seen him. More than serious. Grim.

Something inside plunged. Her defences rose. After yesterday she'd thought her trust in Damen had hit rock bottom. Surely he wasn't going to disappoint her again. She didn't think her bruised heart could bear it.

'A proposition?' She sat straighter, breathing carefully to slow her racing heart. 'You're not going to propose buying my child from me, are you?'

Damen inhabited a world far removed from hers. He had incredible power and money.

Damen's hand closed around her fist. '*Our* child needs both of us, Stephanie. You and me together. As its mother, you hold a very special place no one else can fill.'

Steph sank back in her chair, relief filling her. She'd got him so wrong.

Excitement rippled through her. He'd called her special, said their baby needed them both.

Tendrils of hope wound through her. She loved this man and she knew he...liked her. He was attracted. Now he spoke with respect in his voice about her being special.

Was he beginning to feel a little of what she did? Not love, but perhaps one day he'd assess his feelings and realise—

'What's your proposition?' She needed to hear, not try to guess.

Steph told herself to be calm, not to expect too much. Yet she couldn't stifle a jitter of excitement.

'That you stay in Greece, with me.' He halted, surveying her closely.

Had he registered her suddenly indrawn breath? At least he couldn't feel her fluttering pulse.

'You want me to live in Greece?'

'With me, Stephanie.' His thumb stroked the tender flesh at her wrist. Maybe, after all, he was aware of her runaway heartbeat. 'I want to marry you.'

She froze, unable to speak or even, it seemed, breathe. Her chest tightened from lack of oxygen as she stared across at Damen.

He meant it. She'd never seen him look so serious. In fact, he was frowning. New lines bracketed his mouth and his jaw was a study in tension.

Steph swallowed but couldn't dislodge the blockage in her throat.

This was when he'd tell her he didn't want to lose her. That she'd come to mean so much to him. That together, with time and a common cause in bringing up their child, they might find love.

Steph waited.

Damen's eyes met hers but there was a curious blankness in them, so different from the heat she was used to, or the charming devilry. The lines around his mouth became grooves, carving deeper as she watched.

Was he nervous? No. This wasn't the expression of a man holding his breath as he waited his beloved's response.

'You don't look happy at the idea.'

His shoulders lifted. 'This is a serious matter. It's not about happiness but doing right.' Then, as if reading her expression, he added, 'Happiness will come through our child.' He curved his lips into a smile but it didn't reassure. His face looked tight, painfully so, as if the stretched lips made his face ache.

Disappointment tasted bitter on her tongue. Disappointment and dismay.

She'd imagined that a proposal of marriage would be a happy event.

Not this one. Not with the would-be groom looking as if he tasted poison. Even his golden tan had paled. He looked almost unwell.

A proposition, he'd called it. Not a proposal.

As if this was a business deal.

'Why marry?' she eventually croaked.

Damen looked down to their joined hands. 'Many reasons. Above all, to do what's best for our baby. Children thrive in a stable home, loved by their family. We can give the baby that. I will love our child with all that I am, and I believe you feel the same.'

Piercing green eyes snared hers and Steph nodded. Already she felt protective of this new life. Soon, she guessed, it would become love.

'If we marry we can give it the support and stability it needs. We can support each other, and our families will too. Your grandmother, my mother and sisters. I'll fly your grandmother to Greece as often as she likes. Who knows, she may even settle here once you're living in the country.'

Steph tried to imagine Gran in Greece. It was generous of Damen to think of her, to realise Steph would want her support.

'I want the best for our child, Stephanie. Sharing the burdens and joys of parenthood is not only fair but also the best outcome for all of us.'

It sounded as if he was speaking about a commercial merger, not a family.

'I know it's a big thing to move to a new country. But we'll visit Australia often. If you want to pursue your business here, I'll back you, give you every support. Plus we'll travel.' His hand squeezed hers. 'That's your dream. I can make that happen. We'll go wherever you want.' He stopped and she saw calculation in his expression. 'That's the benefit of marrying a wealthy man. I can provide whatever you want.'

Except love.

Except being wanted for myself, not because of my baby.

A great hollow formed in her middle, expanding wider

and deeper till it felt as if she was nothing but a narrow layer of flesh over gaping emptiness.

Questions crowded. Why did he want marriage so badly when he must know he'd already have rights as a father? What if it didn't work? What if Damen fell in love with someone else? For as sure as her name was Logan, he wasn't in love with her.

Soon, she knew, the hurt would start.

It was starting now as she stared into a face set with determination yet almost gaunt with…what? Damen looked ill.

His proposition sounded like a company merger.

A merger he doesn't really want.

As soon as the thought rose Steph knew it was right.

He offered marriage to stake a claim for complete access to the baby.

'You really want this child,' she murmured and had immediate confirmation from the flash of excitement in his eyes.

'Absolutely!'

Steph's insides churned in distress.

He wants the child but not you.

He doesn't want marriage but he'll go through with it to secure his baby.

'I'm sorry, Damen, I—'

'Don't make up your mind now!'

'I was about to say I need time to think.'

'Fine. Excellent.'

But it wasn't fine and it certainly wasn't excellent. Steph's heart had cracked and she feared that soon it might just shatter.

CHAPTER THIRTEEN

DAMEN HAD LEARNED to rein in impatience. Even as a CEO he occasionally had to bide his time, wait for the right moment to seal a deal.

This was one of those times. Stephanie was coming to terms with her pregnancy. She wasn't her usual bright, forthright self. Even allowing for shock and the life changes she faced, he worried at her lacklustre mood.

His own mood was best not examined. He got through each day focusing on what needed to be done.

He'd begun searching for a family home. An island within commuting distance. Somewhere with a private beach and large garden. Stephanie might like overseeing the renovations. Or perhaps they'd build. That could be the project to drag her out of the doldrums.

Damen devoted himself to persuading her to accept him by showing her how good life would be for her here.

He spirited her away for an overnight stay on picturesque Hydra. In Athens he took her not to crowded social events, but to his favourite restaurants where the food was exquisite and the ambience delightful.

Knowing her interest in his country's culture, he organised a special night visit to the Benaki Museum, a jewel in the crown of Athens' attractions, where the curator led them on a private tour. For the first time in days Stephanie was animated, inspecting exquisite ancient gold jewellery, hand-stitched traditional clothes and embroideries, art works and other treasures.

He thought about buying her lavish gifts, jewellery and clothes, a car, but decided to wait. He sensed gifts wouldn't sway her.

But what would?

What would make her say yes?

After days of Stephanie avoiding meaningful discussions, the time had come. Damen needed an answer. He was strung so tight at the looming prospect of marriage that it felt as if he might just snap. He barely slept and when he did he was haunted by dreams.

He found her burrowed into the corner of a sofa, a magazine on her lap.

'We need to talk, Stephanie.'

Her head came up as he took a seat opposite, and that was when Damen saw the phone at her ear.

'I have to go, Emma,' she said into the phone. 'I'll call later. I'm fine, truly.' She ended the call, eyes wary. 'What is it, Damen?'

Her eyes were shadowed. She didn't appear like a woman excited to spend her life with him.

His gut clenched. He didn't want marriage either, yet he *needed* it. He *had* to persuade her.

'You haven't given me an answer.' Damen made his voice gentle. He even managed an encouraging smile.

She stared back with unwavering eyes. Her gaze drilled right through him.

'You don't really want to marry me.'

Damen sat taller. 'Of course I do! I proposed, didn't I?'

The words were less than persuasive but she'd caught him off guard. He felt himself floundering.

'That wasn't a marriage proposal, it was a business proposition.'

Was that where he'd gone wrong? Did she want flowers and candles? The trappings of romance? He delved into his pocket and brought out the ring box that had weighed him down for days. He should have produced it earlier.

He was extending his hand when she shook her head and jumped up from the sofa.

'No! Don't.'

Damen frowned. She sounded distressed, as if he'd offered her an insult instead of an honourable proposal.

He shot to his feet.

'Stephanie. *Koritsi mou.* I *do* want to marry you. To make a family for our child.'

Vehemently she shook her head 'That's just it, Damen. You're only interested in the baby. You're not even interested in sex, just fussing over me because I'm carrying your precious heir.'

He stepped forward, the ache in his chest easing. Is that what worried her? 'I've been putting your needs ahead of my own. I—'

'It's more than that.' She heaved a deep breath. 'For days I've watched you. Just as I watched you when you made your...proposition. And one thing is absolutely clear. You don't want to marry me. You looked sick to the stomach when you proposed. Even now you're unhappy. You're not an eager bridegroom.'

That was what made her hesitate?

For the first time ever Damen wished he could lie with ease. Over the years he'd become adept at hiding his feelings, but when it came to marriage the very thought scraped him raw.

'I do want to marry you, Stephanie.' Couldn't she hear the urgency in his voice?

'No, you want control over our baby. You don't want me to leave with it.'

Damen's breath snared. If she knew that, then why hadn't she walked away? She wasn't happy but she hadn't left. Which meant he had a chance to get what he wanted.

His brow corrugated. He was fumbling in the dark, missing the clue that would unlock this situation.

'This isn't about control, Stephanie. This is about caring, building a future.'

She folded her arms, the gesture both protective and defiant. 'But you don't really want marriage, or me.'

Damen's jaw jammed. They were going in circles. Of course he didn't want marriage. The very word was associated in his mind with tragedy and guilt. But he'd do what was right.

'Stephanie…' his voice sounded stretched too thin '… you're wrong. That's exactly what I want.'

'Prove it. Explain why you never intended to marry. Tell me what happened to make you look sick whenever you mention marriage.'

'I don't—'

'I need the truth, Damen. Don't you see?' Her mouth crumpled, her distress stabbing him. 'How can I trust you when there's a problem but you won't acknowledge it? How can I spend my life with you? Be honest and I can decide what to do. Tell me what happened to you.'

Her words shook him to the core.

It was one thing, an appallingly difficult thing, to speak of marriage. It was another, he discovered, to share the secret that darkened his soul.

Yet if he didn't she might leave and never come back.

He dragged air into constricted lungs and gestured to the sofa. 'You should sit.' He waited till she was settled then forced himself to follow suit. What he really wanted was to walk away and not have this conversation.

'I almost married once.' His tone was clipped. 'I was twenty-two and in love. Ingrid was…' he paused '…perfect.' He breathed out the word.

'Or so I thought.' He caught Stephanie's sombre stare. 'She was beautiful and engaging. Clever, great company.' Great in bed.

At least he'd thought so. Now he had trouble remembering sexual pleasure with her. His mind was too full of Stephanie.

'What went wrong?'

'My father advised me to wait but I was young and impatient, so sure of myself.' His next breath felt like millstones grinding in his chest.

'You ignored him?'

'I listened but I wasn't convinced. Then, a week before the wedding, I found her phone. Not her usual phone but a spare I knew nothing about. I picked it up thinking to leave a surprise message but I was the one to get the surprise.'

Damen looked away, his thoughts a decade in the past.

'I found messages between her and her boyfriend.'

He heard a gasp.

'I thought it was a joke but I couldn't let it go. I dug deeper. It turned out she had a boyfriend when she met me. Our great romantic love was a calculated scheme to get their hands on my money. Even with a prenup there was a sizeable profit to be had if she left me after a year. Plus anything she'd managed to siphon off in the meantime.'

Ingrid had been good at that, convincing him to splash the cash on her. On things with a solid resale value, like jewellery.

'She was going to marry you then take your money to her lover?' Stephanie's tone was breathless.

'Exactly.' He darted a look her way.

'But she didn't get it...you.'

'I dumped her five days before the wedding.'

'Good! You were well rid of her.' The spark in Stephanie's eyes might have cheered him in other circumstances.

'That's not all.' Damen looked at the doors to the terrace. The impulse to escape was almost unstoppable. But she needed to hear this. 'My father called me into his office. He was...severely disappointed.' Damen's mouth twisted, remembering his normally placid father's tirade about staining the family honour and what a disappointment his only son was.

Damen looked down at his linked hands, the movement pulling the muscles in his neck too tight.

'He wouldn't let me explain, just launched into a diatribe

about how I wasn't fit to bear the Nicolaides name. How close he was to disowning me for dishonouring my fiancée and creating a scandal. I, being young and proud and hating that I hadn't taken his original advice, just stood there, getting angrier and more outraged. How dared he berate *me* when Ingrid was a liar? How could he take her part without asking my side of things? I didn't rush to disabuse him. I let him rant, knowing he'd have to eat his words when he learned the truth.'

'But he calmed down when you told him.'

Damen lifted his head. His body felt leaden, each movement ponderous. Even sucking air into his chest was an effort.

'No.' Damen swallowed. The knot of terrible emotion rose from his chest to his throat, threatening to choke him. 'Before I'd even started explaining he collapsed. The scene brought on a massive heart attack. He died before the medics arrived. I tried CPR but…'

Damen looked into Stephanie's pale face but it wasn't hers he saw.

'He died because of me. I'm to blame for my father's death.'

He sucked in a breath that didn't ease the cramping pain in his chest.

'Of course I feel sick when I think of marriage. It makes me remember a death that could have been avoided. My actions destroyed my father and my whole family paid the price.'

Stephanie reeled. Damen's anguish shattered her lingering anger and disappointment. He looked like a man crushed under an impossible weight, his features stark with pain, his voice unrecognisable.

She stumbled up, her instinct to comfort him. She couldn't bear to see him so tortured. But she'd only taken one step when Damen flung out an arm to ward her off.

She stopped, heart contracting. That gesture said so much. About his hurt. And his ability to hurt her, more, it seemed, every day.

'Damen, you can't take responsibility for your father's death. There must have been an underlying condition—'

'Didn't you hear what I said?' He shot to his feet but turned away, not towards her. His shoulders hunched as he shoved his hands in his pockets. 'It happened because of my actions. There's no changing that.' He paused. 'So now you know. Are you satisfied?'

Steph stared at that proud, handsome profile set in obdurate lines. Her heart bled for him. Yet the taut way he held himself confirmed his mind was closed.

For one heartbeat, then another, she stood poised to go to him. Comfort him.

Till he turned his back as if to stare at the city view. The discussion was over.

Finally Steph stumbled from the room. With each step she ached for Damen's touch on her arm, the sound of him calling her back.

There was nothing.

Hours later she sat in the shade of a spreading tree in the ruins of the city's ancient marketplace. Before her was a marble temple but she didn't see its beautiful symmetry. Instead she saw the anguish in Damen's eyes, heard the rasp of guilt and regret in his voice.

He believed he'd killed his father. It seemed the terrible events of that time, his fiancée's betrayal and guilt over his father's death, had melded in his mind. He saw his marriage plans as a catalyst for disaster. No wonder he'd planned never to marry.

That explained his nightmares, calling out to his father.

Sympathy knotted Steph's insides. She'd hung on to disappointment because she sensed his proposal was reluctant.

Now indignation and anger transformed into pity. What a burden Damen carried!

She wanted to wrap her arms around him and comfort him. She wanted the right to be at his side.

She loved him.

Instead of happiness the knowledge brought pain.

At least now she understood it was the idea of marriage itself that sickened him.

It wasn't anything personal.

That was the problem. None of Damen's plans for her was personal. He didn't want *her*. He wanted their baby. Tying her to him in marriage guaranteed that.

She doubled up in distress. It would be cruel to abandon him, knowing the past tortured him. But how much crueller to her child to stay, living a lie that might end in heartache for everyone?

Could she accept his proposal and hope marriage might lead Damen to love rather than to boredom or dislike?

Or should she make a clean break?

'And so,' she paused to twist her goblet of sparkling water, 'I've decided to go home, to Australia.'

The words pounded into Damen like sledgehammer blows.

He wished he hadn't eaten his delicious dinner. It curdled in his stomach.

'But I'll stay till the end of our two months.' Her lips formed something approximating a smile. 'I'll honour our contract.'

Damen shoved his chair back from the table, the legs screeching on the flagstones of the rooftop terrace. But instead of shooting to his feet he reached for Stephanie's hand.

Touching her silky skin eased his rackety heartbeat.

It had been an emotional day. He'd plumbed the depths with his admission. Yet in the face of this the burden he'd carried for a decade faded towards insignificance. He'd learned to cope with guilt. He sensed he wouldn't cope with Stephanie leaving.

The world blurred as his heart beat too fast and the edges of his vision blackened. He saw her eyes widen.

Damen focused on keeping his hand gentle on hers while the rest of his body went rigid.

All except for that bit of him deep within that crumbled at her words.

Stephanie leaving him.

The thought was unbearable.

Stephanie living on the other side of the world. Taking their baby.

He'd be reduced to seeing his child for, at best, six months a year. As for Stephanie... He imagined cursory conversations as the child passed from one to the other. They'd be strangers, living separate lives.

That odd feeling intensified. As if bits of his organs, his bones, broke away. Roaring white noise filled his head. Reality reduced to the racing thrum of his heart and the hand so soft and unresponsive beneath his.

Arguments to make her stay formed in his head. Inducements that only extreme wealth could buy.

Yet, as he looked into those earnest eyes, read the downward turn of her mouth and the fluttering pulse beneath his hand, Damen knew he was beaten.

Nothing he could offer, neither money nor privilege, would buy her company.

Devastation filled him.

Yet he had to ask. 'Is there anything I can do to change your mind?'

Her mouth crimped at the corners as if she bit back an instinctive response. For a second her eyes blazed more gold than brown. Then they shuttered.

'Nothing.'

CHAPTER FOURTEEN

DAYS LATER, DAMEN stood before his mother in the comfortable sitting room of her Athens home.

His world had tilted on its axis since Stephanie had forced him to reveal his dreadful secret, then declared she was going back to Australia.

Her decision had left him, for the second time in his life, feeling utterly powerless.

Who could blame her for choosing to go? Why would she tie herself to a man who'd killed his own father?

The pain wrapping around his chest worsened daily, as if unseen bonds tightened with each passing hour.

Now Damen had one more trial to face. He couldn't make things right for his father or for Stephanie, couldn't convince her to stay. Yet the unquiet past still haunted him. He'd been a coward in not speaking the truth before. It was a truth he owed his mother.

Yet speaking the words, watching comprehension dawn on her beloved face, made his heart break.

'Damen, no! It's not true!' Her voice shook.

Damen stood his ground, hands clasped behind his back.

'I'm sorry, Mama. But it is. Ten years ago I told you a sanitised version of what happened.'

He moved towards her as she scrambled from her seat, taking her trembling hands.

'You were distraught. I didn't think you'd cope with the whole truth. That *I* was responsible for *Baba's* death. Later...' he sighed. 'Later I was a coward. I couldn't bear to hurt you even more.'

'Foolish, foolish boy.' To his amazement she leaned against him, letting him embrace her. His heart catapulted against his ribs. He'd feared her reaction. Yet still he was gripped by a terrible tension.

His mother leaned back in his arms, her eyes locking on his. 'You're wrong. You didn't kill your father.' Her voice cracked and she squeezed his arm.

Damen shook his head, pain shafting through his soul. Of course his mother didn't want to believe it.

'I'm sorry, Mama.' His breath lifted his chest. 'I didn't listen to him earlier when I should have. Then, that final day, I let him rant because I was too proud, too hurt that he blamed me.'

'He wasn't himself,' she answered. 'He was stressed about the business—'

'That doesn't excuse me.'

His mother shook her head, her expression wistful. 'Your father was a good man but he wasn't himself. He was... scared.'

'Scared?' Damen's head reared back. He couldn't believe such a thing of his father.

'I wanted to tell you but he was adamant. He was scared for the business. Times were tough and you were relatively inexperienced. He had faith in you,' she said quickly, 'but he feared you had a lot to learn if you had to take over.'

'But—' He stopped when she raised her hand.

'He was moody, seeing disaster everywhere, which wasn't your father.' Her expression was wistful. 'You know how positive he usually was. But the doctors warned his health was bad and told him to step back from work. He'd already had two heart attacks.'

'Two heart attacks?' Damen goggled. How had he not known?

'I'm sorry. I wanted him to tell you and your sisters but he refused. They were mild attacks but he was told to work less and get more exercise. He promised he would but instead he put in extra hours, wanting to fix some problems before he handed over to you.'

'He never mentioned me taking over. Never mentioned being ill.'

'He was going to talk to you after the wedding.' She dabbed her eyes. 'He wanted to hand Nicolaides Shipping to you in good shape, but with the economic troubles...' She shrugged. 'You weren't responsible. He'd promised to reduce his hours but he was obsessed with fixing the business first. I tried to persuade him—'

'It's not your fault, Mama.'

'And it's not yours. You said he was ranting. You know how out of character that was. The stress got to him, the worry he wouldn't be around to support you and your sisters.' She bit her lip. 'If anyone caused the attack, it was him. Ignoring medical advice.'

His mother blinked back tears and Damen pulled her close, murmuring words of comfort.

His head spun. If what his mother said was true...

Of course it was. She'd never invent something like that.

It didn't excuse his stupid behaviour, putting his pride first, but it changed so much. Gave a new perspective. The revelation of his father's physical and mental state suddenly made sense, explaining his unusual behaviour. It didn't absolve Damen but already the dread weight of guilt eased.

Maybe now he'd learn to cope better with the past.

Was it possible he might even move on from it?

Steph smoothed her hands down the red dress, avoiding her eyes in the mirror. She was afraid her reflection would reveal her pain. Damen had said they were going ashore for a special party. Hopefully this bright colour would divert attention from the smudges beneath her eyes that concealer hadn't quite covered.

She put on the wide silver bangle Damen had given her in Rhodes. The piece was funky and pretty. She'd seen it in an artisan's shop and when Damen bought it for her she'd felt trembling excitement as if she was on the brink of a thrilling new part of her life.

Her breath shuddered. Thrilling, yes, with single motherhood and a broken heart. Not what she'd hoped for.

She'd fallen for a man so damaged by his first love that he was incapable of loving. Or at least loving her. Maybe one day he'd love again, but she'd be gone. She couldn't live with the little he offered. Duty. Responsibility. Never love.

Two weeks ago in Athens she'd announced she was leaving and for a few moments she'd thought there was hope. That he *did* care for her and would fight to keep her. Instead Damen accepted her announcement with soul-destroying equanimity.

All she could do was hope to get through their contracted time with dignity.

Fifteen minutes later she and Damen were on a small island. It was beautiful. Even the water in the bay was jewel-toned. Ahead was a gracious old house. Pale yellow walls, terracotta tiles, long windows with white shutters. It looked charming.

Steph drew a deep breath scented by the sea and wild herbs.

'Who lives here?' She looked for evidence of a party but all was silent.

'It was built a long time ago by a famous admiral.' It was the first time Damen had spoken since they left the yacht and his deep voice trawled through her like honey-dipped silk. 'He was a pirate too, according to the stories. You like it?'

'It's gorgeous.' Easier to concentrate on her surroundings than Damen, close beside her but distant in every way that mattered.

How was she to get through the next weeks? She couldn't leave. They had a deal. It wasn't his fault she'd made the error of falling in love.

Steph's heart squeezed.

They reached the front door and Damen opened it. 'After you.'

Steph stepped into the hallway, blinking after the dazzling sunshine. They were in a square foyer with an elegant curving staircase.

'This way.' Damen ushered her into a sitting room, the furnishings beautiful but worn.

More silence. There were no voices. No clink of china or glass. She looked out to Damen's yacht, moored in the bay. There were no other boats.

Her spine prickled with belated warning.

Steph swung around to find Damen close. His distinctive scent wafted into her nostrils. Her yearning grew. How was she to pretend not to care?

'What is this, Damen?'

'It's the house I've bought. I'll use it as my base and commute to Athens when I need to.' He looked around. 'It needs renovation and a sympathetic extension, but when it's done it will be special.'

Steph agreed but didn't want to discuss renovations.

'There's no party, is there? Why are we here?'

To her surprise Damen smiled. It was the first genuine smile she'd seen from him in two weeks and it unravelled her defences.

'This is a kidnap.'

'Sorry?' She must have misheard.

'I'm kidnapping you. I botched my first effort but this time I'm determined to do it right.' The smile faded and suddenly he was standing so close the heat from his body washed through her. 'I'm keeping you on the island till you agree to my terms.'

Steph tottered backwards, her hand at her throat. 'You can't!'

'Watch me.' He looked more sombre than she'd ever known him.

Tears of fury and hurt pricked her eyes. 'You're utterly

ruthless. What do you want, Damen? Another contract? I can tell you now I'll never sign over my baby to you. I'll swim to the next island if I have to.'

'It's not like that.'

'Of course it's like that. If you think holding me here will convince me to—'

'It's not the baby I want.'

Steph's mouth sagged open.

'Not the baby?'

He was so close she had to tilt her chin to meet his eyes. Awareness zinged through her. She tried to stifle it and focus on anger.

'No, I want *you*.'

'You're not making sense.'

'On the contrary, for the first time since we met I'm talking perfect sense.' His glittering eyes held a promise of something that made her heart turn over. 'I've wanted you since the day we met.'

'You had me, remember?'

He shook his head. 'I've never had you, *agapi mou*, not really. Oh, we had sex, and it was amazing. But I want more than your body.'

'Yes. You want my baby.' She couldn't let herself forget that.

'Of course I want our child. Or, I should say I want to share our child. But there's something I want more.'

Steph frowned, not daring to hope.

'I want *you*, Stephanie. Not just sleeping in my bed or sharing responsibility for our child.' He paused and she saw his nostrils flare as if he fought for breath. 'I want you with me because you care for me. Because I care for you.' Another pause. Another deep breath.

'I love you, Stephanie. If you give us a chance, I believe I can make you happy. You might even come to love me too.'

Steph shuffled back till she came up against a sofa. 'You're lying. You don't…love me.' Her heart dipped on the word and she wrapped her arms around her middle to keep the hurt at bay. 'You're cruel pretending to.'

'You accused me of lying before, *agapi mou*, and I regret you had cause ever to doubt my honesty. But I tell you now, on my oath as a Nicolaides, I've never been more genuine. I love you.' He said it again slowly, his gaze pinioning her so she couldn't look away.

'No!' She put out a hand to ward him off, though he hadn't moved. Her palm landed on his chest, her fingers splaying on familiar hard contours. 'You're saying this so I'll marry you and so the baby—'

'Actually, I do want to marry you. I want that more than anything.' Damen's hand closed on hers, holding it against his staccato-beating heart. His eyes gleamed as if lit by an inner fire. 'The thought of losing you has cured me of my horror of marriage. Because I've realised life is too short to waste a moment of being with the woman I love.'

His words slammed the breath back into her lungs. Her head swam.

'I had a long talk with my mother too. I told her about the day my father died. What I hadn't known was that he'd already had a couple of heart attacks. That doesn't excuse my behaviour, but you were right. I was too ready to blame myself. And stupidly I let that stand in the way of *us*.'

Could there really be an *us*? Steph watched him in amazement, trying to process the change in him.

'I want to be your husband, Stephanie. But if you don't want to marry, I'll accept that. Whatever you like, as long as you stay. Give me a chance to show you how good our life can be together.'

Steph blinked, overwhelmed. She wanted so much to believe but she couldn't let herself.

'I was attracted to you from the first. I only left because I thought I'd wrecked my chances with you. Then in Corfu…' He paused and she felt his heart quicken beneath her palm. 'You have no idea how much I wanted you. Even if I hadn't needed a pretend lover I'd have tried to seduce you. Everything about you attracted me. Your looks, your feisty attitude, your sense of humour. Even the way you refused to be impressed by me. You sizzle with energy and passion and I wanted that for myself. I still do. Especially now I've learned what a warm and honest heart you have.'

Steph's breath came in short bursts, warring emotions filling her. His words meant so much, and she desperately wanted to believe them.

'You didn't love me a fortnight ago. You didn't want to marry me.' His unwilling proposal had hurt so badly.

Damen lifted his other hand to her cheek, and to her shame she didn't have the strength to shy away. If anything she nestled closer.

Damen's pupils dilated. His fingers moved in a tender caress.

'That's just it. I *did* love you, though I hadn't let myself think in those terms. Because I'd loved Ingrid and that led to heartache and tragedy.'

'It wasn't your fault!' She'd felt helpless, watching Damen grapple with his demons. 'Stop blaming yourself.'

'That's what my mother says.'

'She's right.' Steph hoped never to see such anguish as she'd seen in Damen's eyes that day.

'I'm glad you think so. She also told me I was a fool if I let you go without telling you how I feel.'

Steph's eyes widened, hope rising.

'But I was going to tell you anyway. I can't let you go because I love you. Not as I thought I loved Ingrid, with a boy's infatuation, but deeply, with all I am and all I hope to be.' His voice deepened on the words. They sounded like a pledge. '*S'agapo,* Stephanie *mou.*'

'Oh, Damen.' She blinked back tears. 'How am I supposed to stay strong and resist you when you say that?'

'I want you to be strong, *asteri mou.* To be the independent, gorgeous woman you already are. I just don't want you to resist *me*.' His voice cracked and her eyes widened. 'Stay with me. Things were good between us and they can be even better. Look in your heart and give us a chance. Maybe you'll come to love me too.'

The last of Steph's resistance crumbled. She'd taken chances and made mistakes. But this wasn't a mistake.

This was the man she wanted to build a life with. A man who'd wrestled his demons and emerged wanting her. A decent, caring, wonderful man who deserved a second chance.

In the end the words slipped out easily.

'I already love you, Damen. That's why I've been miserable, thinking all you cared about was our baby.'

She felt the crash of his heart at her words.

He must have seen the truth in her face, for he smiled. That soul-lifting smile that made her heart beat double time.

'You love me.' His voice held wonder and satisfaction.

His arm looped around her waist, pulling her to him.

Steph went willingly.

'And you love me.' It was there in his eyes, his embrace, in the very air they breathed.

'Let me show you how much.' His arms were strong yet gentle as he scooped her up and headed for the staircase and the bedrooms above. 'I'll never tire of saying the words, *agapi mou*, but I want you to be absolutely sure of my feelings, and actions speak louder than words.'

In the end he convinced Stephanie both with words and potently persuasive actions.

EPILOGUE

A COOL BREEZE ruffled the cypresses but the sky was cloudless and the day perfect.

Damen's gaze traversed the garden from the villa, across the terrace where friends and family clustered. The steps to this garden by the sea were bright with potted roses and other flowers in shades of red, Stephanie's favourite colour. Red ribbons decorated the arbour where he stood with Christo.

Damen didn't care about decorations. Nor witnesses, though he was glad his family was here. His sisters gossiped with Clio. Manos and his wife chatted with friends and kids raced in circles, laughing as parents herded them to seats. His mother sat with Stephanie's grandmother and the friend she'd brought from Australia, a tall, white-haired man. From the older man's expression when he looked at Mrs Logan, Damen guessed there'd be another wedding soon.

'Emma's done a fantastic job preparing for today.' Damen mightn't care about decorations but he wanted today perfect for Stephanie.

'I'll tell her you said so,' Christo responded. 'She'll be thrilled. Even more thrilled than when you said you wanted to be married on Corfu.'

'It's a special place for us.' Where he and Stephanie had met again, argued and struck sparks off each other, and agreed to become pretend lovers. Now they were so much more. 'Besides, the renovations aren't finished at our villa.'

'You can have the christening party there.'

Damen met his friend's grin just as the string quartet began playing a familiar tune. His heart shot straight to his throat, beating hard and fast.

He turned and his breath stopped.

She was even more beautiful than he remembered. He hadn't seen her since yesterday, having stayed aboard the yacht while she spent the night with Emma.

Damen's throat dried.

Stephanie's hair shone like ebony and she carried red flowers before her small baby bump. Her gown was deep cream, wide across the shoulders but fitted across the breasts and falling in folds to her feet. The pearl and ruby necklace he'd given her glowed against her skin. She looked as elegant as a princess, as delicate as a fairy. She was his dream of heaven.

Then she was there, before him. Her eyes shone golden brown, her smile turned him inside out.

Damen took her hand, lifting it to his mouth. The scent of vanilla and Stephanie, of happiness, filled him.

He whispered in her ear, 'You're absolutely sure?' He'd suggested that they marry after the baby was born, a gesture to prove he wanted marriage because he loved her, not to secure their child.

'I'm sure.' Her eyes flashed. 'I can't wait to be your wife. I love you, Damen Nicolaides, and I mean to have you.'

Damen grinned as his heart filled. 'Have I mentioned I adore a woman who knows what she wants?'

Ignoring custom, he swooped down to kiss her lips. Instantly she melted, his fiery, adorable love.

The sound of Christo clearing his throat finally penetrated and reluctantly Damen straightened. Stephanie's eyes shone and a tantalising smile curved her sweet lips. Damen took her arm and turned to the celebrant.

Could any day be more perfect?

And this was just the beginning.

* * * * *

LET'S TALK

Romance

For exclusive extracts, competitions and special offers, find us online:

- facebook.com/millsandboon
- @millsandboonuk
- @millsandboon

Or get in touch on 0844 844 1351*

For all the latest titles coming soon, visit millsandboon.co.uk/nextmonth